FIRE GAMES

A CHRISTIAN SUSPENSE AND ROMANCE

LORANA HOOPES

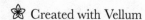

NOTE FROM THE AUTHOR

Thank you so much for picking up this book. Though this was originally going to be titled The Cop's Fiery Bride, the suspense made me feel as if it needed a new look. Therefore, I decided to turn it into a spin off series. I hope you like this book. If you do, please leave a review at your retailer. It really does make a difference because it lets people make an informed decision about books.

If you are reading this book, you also qualify for a special bonus. Simply email your receipt or the first word of chapter 10 to loranahoopes@gmail.com and I'll send you a short PDF of Cassidy's time on the reality show. Just my way of saying thank you.

Sign up for Lorana Hoopes's newsletter and get her book, The Billionaire's Impromptu Bet, as a welcome gift. Get Started Now!

CHAPTER 1

Cassidy Marcel gazed at the firehouse with trepidation. She loved her job, but she also knew firefighters. They loved to razz each other over everything, and her appearance on the reality dating show, Who Wants to Marry a Cowboy, would be no exception.

She'd gone on the show at the urging of her mother who was begging for grandkids, but Cassidy couldn't deny her biological clock was ticking as well. And it had come on suddenly. One day, she'd been content to be a single woman focusing on her career as a firefighter and the next, a desperate need to start a family had erupted within her. She'd begun dating again, but none of the men she had been out with fit the bill of what she was looking for – stable, self-sufficient, and a man of God.

So, when she'd seen that Tyler, the cowboy bachelor for this episode, was one, she'd re-considered her initial refusal and asked God for clarity. While she hadn't heard a loud voice in her head, she'd felt a sense of peace about it, and so she'd done the audition. And been chosen. And even felt a connection with Tyler. Until it became obvious that he had eyes for someone else. Now, she was back with a wounded ego, a bruised heart, and a feeling of confusion as she wondered if she'd been following her own will instead of God's. And she knew there would be teasing from her fellow firefighters.

Plus, she wondered how Captain Fitzgerald was going to react. The stony-faced Captain hadn't been her biggest fan before she took three weeks off; she assumed she would be even lower on his list now.

Inhaling deeply, she pulled her shoulders back hoping she appeared more confident than she felt. Then she opened her car door, tucked her dark hair behind her ears, and walked into the lion's den.

"Marcel, so glad you could grace us with your presence again." Billy Campbell, or Bubba, as everyone called him stood before her, a giant smile on his face. He was one of her favorite people in the firehouse. Originally from Texas, he had a heart bigger than his smile and was more like an older brother than a co-worker. "I didn't want you to feel like we didn't want you, so I thought this might help." From behind his back, he brandished a miniature black cowboy hat and held it out to her. Though small, it somehow sported sequins that caught and shimmered in the light.

Cassidy rolled her eyes good naturedly as she shook her head. She should have expected something like this, especially after the sugar incident last year. When Cassidy first joined the firehouse, they had celebrated by taking her out to a local dive that served decent food and boasted a karaoke night. None of her favorites had been available though, and Cassidy ended up singing Def Leopard's "Pour Some Sugar on Me." The next day, the guys had all presented her with bags of sugar throughout the day. Sugar wouldn't have to grace her grocery list for another six months at least.

"Haha, thanks, Bubba. I missed you too." She grabbed the hat knowing several more of these would be in store before the day was through. "Did I miss any excitement while I was gone?"

Bubba pushed open the door to the common room that doubled as a living room and the kitchen area. "Only if you count Luca's boycott of Deacon's Paleo meal plan."

"It's not a meal if there are no potatoes in it," Luca said speaking up from the couch. Luca was a Southern boy as well, and he believed every meal should include meat and potatoes. And chocolate. The man insisted that every meal come with a dessert which explained the extra twenty pounds he carried on his frame. Somehow though it didn't hinder him in his job. He was strong and agile and quicker than almost all of them. His eyes flicked up briefly from the television he was watching. "Oh, hey, Marcel, welcome back." He launched something at her without ever taking his eyes off the screen.

She knew what it was before it landed a few inches from her. Another miniature cowboy hat. This one was brown and had a tiny feather. Cassidy picked it up and flashed Luca a crooked grin. "Thanks, Luca. I missed you too."

"Forgive him. He didn't like the brownies I gave him with dinner last night, and he's still sour about it," Deacon said as he stepped around the island in the kitchen and toward her and Bubba. Strong and dark skinned, Deacon was the epitome of an oxymoron. His bulging muscles gave him an intimidating presence, but inside he was the biggest teddy bear. He pulled her in for a hug before brandishing his own miniature hat.

Cassidy chuckled as she took the hat though she had no idea what she was going to do with all of these. Though she had received a hat every time Tyler chose her to stay, the producers took them back afterwards to have for the next show. They had allowed her to keep the final hat as a souvenir, and though Cassidy wasn't sure she wanted to remember the show, she kept it as a reminder to never do something like that again.

"Brownies don't have prunes in them," Luca spoke up from the couch.

Cassidy lifted a brow at Deacon. "You made brownies with prunes? Things really have changed in a month." It wasn't that prunes were completely out of the norm for Deacon. He regarded his body as a temple and rarely put anything processed in it, but he also wasn't one for sweets generally. He focused more on macronutrients and desserts rarely fit in his plan.

Deacon shrugged. "I thought I could slip some healthy desserts in on these guys. Keep them a little trimmer in the middle if you know what I mean." He patted his rock-hard abs.

"Might have worked too, if you hadn't eaten them as well," Bubba said with a deep laugh. "That was clue number one they had to be healthy. You really couldn't taste the prunes though, but man did they wreak havoc on my insides later."

"Okay, enough of that," Cassidy said shaking her head and squeezing her eyes shut. The image of a run on the bathroom was not the visual she wanted to have of her fellow firemen.

"Cassidy, oh my gosh, I'm so glad you're back."

Cassidy would have recognized Ivy's voice anywhere.

Not only was she the only other woman in the firehouse, but her voice held just the slightest valley girl twang. On anyone else it might have been annoying, but Ivy was wholesomely sweet, down to earth, and as cute as a button. Her blonde hair perfectly framed her heart-shaped face, and big blue eyes sat above a perfectly-shaped nose that contained no trace of freckles, unlike Cassidy's.

Because Fire Beach wasn't a huge city, it made more sense to have the paramedics and the firefighters housed in the same place, so Ivy was often at the firehouse when Cassidy was. Dispatch usually sent both a firetruck and an ambulance to most calls though medical only calls were increasing which sent Ivy and the other paramedic out at other times as well.

Ivy attacked her with a hug before Cassidy was ready and the gesture jostled her full arms sending the tiny hats flying to the floor. Ivy's eyes widened as she released Cassidy and her petite hand flew to her mouth. "I'm so sorry. I was just so excited to see you. You don't know how awful it's been being the only woman here for the last month." She dropped to the floor to help Cassidy pick up the hats.

Ivy was teasing. Mostly. But Cassidy had been at the firehouse before Ivy arrived, and she remembered how hard it was being the only female. The guys didn't try to make her feel uncomfortable, but men and women were different. She'd been glad when Ivy joined to have another woman to talk to. "Don't worry about it. They're just silly hats, and I'm sorry I left you high and dry."

"Marcel? Is that you?"

Cassidy froze at the stern sound of her captain's voice. Having been recently promoted, Captain Darryl Fitzgerald was now all business. Every rule needed to be followed to the letter, and the teasing shut down when he was around. She snatched the hat and stood. "Good morning, Captain, what can I do for you?"

"You can follow me to my office. We need to have a chat."

"Of course, sir." Cassidy fought the anxiety clawing at her throat. Captain Fitzgerald was intimidating, but she had just returned. She couldn't have done anything too bad. Maybe it was about the hats. She would explain that the guys were just razzing her a little and then take them to her car so they were out of sight.

Cassidy's anxiety increased when Captain Fitzgerald shut the door to his office behind her. Closed door meetings rarely held a good outcome. Her hand rubbed the back of her neck. "Have I done something, sir?" She hated the slight tremble in her voice, but he controlled her future, and she loved her job.

"Sit." He pointed at one of the chairs opposite his desk and then walked to his own chair and sat down.

Cassidy sat in the indicated chair and crossed her legs, then uncrossed them and sat straighter.

"I know that you had time saved up for this trip, but I need someone I can rely on in this firehouse." His steely eyes held hers as if daring her to challenge him.

Cassidy swallowed the knot in her throat and lifted her chin, hoping it came across as confidence and not sass. "I understand, sir, and I have no intention of going anywhere else anytime soon."

He leaned back in his chair and folded his arms across his chest. "That is good to hear, but to be sure, I am giving you some extra cleaning duties. You'll be in charge of cleaning the truck for the next month, and I want it sparkling at the end of every shift. Is that clear?"

Cassidy's mouth fell open, and she hurried to close it. She had no idea if he had the power to do that since she technically had done nothing wrong, but she wasn't going to argue with him. She loved this job and this house. No way did she want to go back to being a floater, so if he wanted her to wash the truck every day, she would do it. If he wanted to put her on kitchen duty, she would do that too even though her cooking left a lot to be desired. "Crystal clear, sir. I promise I am committed to this job and will do whatever it takes to prove it to you."

"Perfect, now we should discuss the mail situation."

He steepled his fingers and regarded her with another cool stare. She was definitely on his list.

She furrowed her brow, confused as to what he could mean. "I'm sorry, the what?"

His eyebrow inched up his forehead. "You don't know?" Cassidy shook her head. "It appears you garnered a few fans while you were gallivanting on your show, and as they didn't know where you lived, they dropped your mail here."

Cassidy winced and bit the inside of her lip. No wonder he was angry. Captain Fitzgerald hated it when anything from the outside encroached on the sanctity of the fire house. "I had no idea, sir. I'm so sorry."

He waved a hand dismissing her. "It is what it is, but I want them gone from the firehouse at the end of your shift."

"Of course, sir. Um, where are they?"

He nodded to the corner of the room, and Cassidy turned spying a large brown bag that she hadn't noticed when they entered. Roughly the size of a burlap sack, it bulged and protruded as wide as appeared possible. "All of that is for me?"

"Yep, letters, gifts, you name it. I *suggest* you find a better place for it."

"Yes, sir." Cassidy pulled her shoulders back as she faced the mountainous bag. Since shift had just started, she might as well take it to the bunk room and go through it while there was time. She didn't need all of this cluttering her small apartment either.

The bag proved unwieldy but thankfully just enough extra sack remained at the top that she was able to drag it down the hallway and into the bunk room. Meant generally for sleeping when they worked long shifts, the bunk room held rows of two beds separated by half walls. A small table that contained only a lamp sat between each two-bed section.

She and Ivy shared the section at the very back of the room, and sweat rolled down Cassidy's spine as she pulled the bag to the bunk she normally slept in. With a sigh, she plopped down on the bunk and opened the bag. If Santa had been real, she would know exactly how he felt. She grabbed one of the envelopes and opened it.

"Dear Cassidy, I saw you on the show, and I think we'd make a great couple. I love horses and roller skating. You can call me at 555-1324. Signed, David. P.S. If a woman answers, it's just my mom."

Cassidy wrinkled her nose, shook her head, and laid the letter to the side. No need to keep that one. She wanted a man established enough that he lived on his own or maybe with a roommate. Rent wasn't cheap in the city, but moms were a no go. She wanted a man who had a good relationship with his mother but who didn't still live with his mother. She reached into the bag again.

One down and only a few hundred to go. It was going to be a long afternoon.

Jordan issued his apology as he hurried into the office. "Sorry I'm late. We were chasing a lead."

"Of course you were," Graham said with a roll of his eyes.

Anger flared inside Jordan, and he lashed out at his brother. "They're missing kids, Graham. I think that's a little more important than whatever Dad may or may not have left us."

Graham held up his hands in surrender and Mr. Keyes, the attorney, cleared his throat as if hoping that might ease the tension in the room.

"It's no problem, Jordan, we were just getting started." Mr. Keyes adjusted his tie before placing his hands on either side of a stack of papers. "I'm sure you know that I called you in today for a reading of your father's will. Most of it is rather straightforward, but there is something I wasn't sure you were aware of." He picked up the top sheet of paper and scanned it before flipping it around to them. "Did you know your father owned a bar?"

"A bar?" Graham asked leaning forward.

"That's not possible. Dad was an alcoholic. Why would he own a bar?" Jordan asked.

"It hasn't been a bar in a long time. In fact, it hasn't been anything for a long time. I drove by the other day, so I would have current information for you both. It appears to be boarded up currently." He pulled a picture from the stack and slid it across the table to Graham who glanced at it before handing it to Jordan.

"So, we should try and sell it, right?" Jordan asked. He had no use for a bar or the rundown building in the picture.

"No, we can't sell it," Graham said shooting him an incredulous look. "Dad obviously kept the bar for a reason."

A reason? Jordan doubted it. Their father had spent most of his life so drunk that he rarely had a reason for anything. "He probably forgot he owned it and therefore had no presence of mind to sell it. What would we do with an old building?"

Mr. Keyes said nothing but shifted his gaze from one brother to the next as they argued.

"What would we do?" Graham turned in his chair to face Jordan, his face a picture of contempt. "We fix it up, give it new life, take it back to how it once was."

Jordan shook his head. Obsessed with focusing on the positive, Graham always wanted to fix things, even when the better option would be to stay out of it. "No way, I'm not opening a bar. I won't encourage drinking and enable the same behavior that claimed Dad."

"Fine, we'll turn it into a family restaurant then. A place where cops can hang out and have a sense of community." Graham had added that last part to try and persuade Jordan but he wasn't biting.

"I have no time to fix up a restaurant. Nor do I know anything about running a restaurant. And what about the money? Did Dad leave any money to fix this place?"

"Your father left you the proceeds from the sale of the house and he had a few stocks and bonds, but it isn't much."

And there it was. Their father hadn't kept the house in good enough condition to turn a profit and he hadn't thought about his sons' future either. He'd only thought about his next drink. "See? It isn't much. Probably not enough to renovate an old bar and turn it into a restaurant."

Graham folded his arms across his chest and turned away from Jordan. "I'm not selling. Dad could have sold the building years ago, and he didn't. That tells me it meant something to him, so I'm going to restore it with or without you."

Jordan turned fierce eyes on the lawyer. "Can he do that? Can he make me keep it?"

Mr. Keyes shrugged and offered an apologetic half

smile. "He could offer to buy you out, but there is no stipulation that he has to sell."

Before he could say anything else, Jordan's phone buzzed. He swiped the screen and shook his head. Another kid had gone missing. "I have to go, but this isn't over. We are going to discuss this, Graham."

CHAPTER 2

*C*assidy blew out another exasperated breath as she surveyed the stacks of envelopes surrounding her. Who knew there were this many lonely men hoping to meet a woman they saw on television? Of course, they weren't all from men. She had gotten quite a few letters from women as well, mostly wishing her luck or telling her they were glad Tyler kept her around for as long as he did. There were even a few from young girls who said they wanted to be firefighters when they grew up too. Those made her smile. Firefighting was still a hard occupation for women to get into, but Cassidy enjoyed seeing the numbers rise each year.

"I was wondering where you went." Ivy's voice carried across the room as she approached. "Whoa, what is all that?"

Cassidy rolled her eyes and fanned her hands out. "This is my fan mail. Want to help?"

Ivy's blue eyes lit up and her smile shone with her exuberance. "Do I ever? I want all the juicy details, and you better not leave anything out." She pushed a few pieces of paper aside as she dropped onto the bed beside Cassidy and grabbed an envelope from the bag.

Normally, she loved sharing details with Ivy – the girls would often rehash their latest dates – but Cassidy didn't want to share the details of this experience. It reminded her too much of grade school when captains chose players for teams and there were always those kids who were chosen last every time. She'd been that kid once and she still remembered how much it hurt hearing every other name called. After that, she'd worked hard to improve her athletic skill so she wouldn't ever be the last one chosen again.

Being on the show had been similar. Her gut had clenched with every ceremony, and she'd sighed with relief when her name was finally called. The difference was, those women had not been her teammates but her competition. Eventually, there would only be one woman remaining, and while Cassidy knew that, she had still opened her heart to Tyler until it became clear he only had eyes for Laney.

"Not much to tell." Cassidy's eyes shifted back to the bag. She wouldn't begrudge the couple their happiness, but it was still a bruise to her ego and an experience she didn't want to relive. "Tyler wasn't really interested in any of us though I think we would have been good together."

Ivy stared at her, and Cassidy knew she was deciding whether to push it or leave the topic alone. Thankfully, she chose the latter. "Would you have moved to Texas for him and left all of this?" Ivy gestured around the room before tearing open an envelope and pulling out a letter.

Immediately, the heavy scent of cologne filled the air, and Ivy's face scrunched in disgust. She held the paper away from her face with one hand and covered her nose with the other. "Whew, I think whoever wrote this used half a bottle of cologne on this letter."

"Ugh." Cassidy waved her hand in front of her nose to try and lessen the stench. Axe. It would have to be Axe. It was her least favorite cologne and seemed to be the one of choice for most of the guys at her gym. The locker rooms always smelled of Axe when a class ended. "Don't even bother reading it. Just toss that one."

Ivy balled the letter up and tossed it across the room. It landed more than five feet from the trash can, but at only five foot three, Ivy wasn't much of a basketball player anyway. She shrugged and flashed a sheepish grin. "We'll get that one later, but I needed some air."

Cassidy took a tentative breath and nearly gagged.

The stench still clung to the air. "We might need to get a fan. That doesn't appear to be dissipating."

"In a minute. First you have to answer my question." Ivy reached into the bag and pulled out another envelope.

"What was the question again?" Cassidy dropped her eyes to the envelope in her hand. She knew the question but was hoping Ivy might have forgotten.

Ivy put her envelope down and cocked an eyebrow at Cassidy putting on her best 'you can't fool me' expression. "You know very well what the question was, missy. Would you have moved and left all of this?"

"I don't know." Cassidy unfolded the letter she had opened and pondered the question. It was a question she had asked herself since she'd heard about the reality show. Her work was here as were her friends and her church, but if finding the perfect man meant moving, then she supposed she would do that too. "I love it here, but I'd also like to get married one day and start a family. If we had connected and that meant moving to Texas, I think I would have."

"You don't have to move all the way to Texas to get married. We have a ton of available men right here in Fire Beach, Illinois." Ivy wiggled her eyebrows suggestively and grinned at Cassidy.

If only that were true. "Yeah, men who want Barbie dolls like you not tomboys like me." Cassidy had never been the one guys flocked to of her friends. Generally, she was the one guys befriended so they could pick her brain and find out about her other friends. Whether it was her thicker stature or her job or her tomboy nature, Cassidy didn't know, but she was tired of being alone. Well, not entirely alone. She had her friends and her church, but those didn't really count. Not in the way she wanted.

"Uh, I think this stack here shows that's not always true." Ivy gestured at the massive pile in front of them and the papers on the bed around them. "I've never gotten paper cuts opening all my fan mail."

"Well, you would if you had been on national television." Actually, Ivy probably would have gotten three times as much fan mail. Cassidy still didn't understand how her friend was single except that she was picky. Every time she found a new man, she also found something wrong with him. She was beginning to wonder if Ivy even wanted a relationship.

Her eyes dropped to the envelope she had pulled out and she scanned the writing as she continued. "So far, there's been nothing worth writing home about in here anyway. I think most of them are lonelier than I am…." Her voice trailed off as she read the letter again.

"What?" Ivy asked clearly picking up on the change in Cassidy's voice.

Cassidy didn't want to read the words out loud. With

a trembling hand, she passed the letter to Ivy who perused it, her eyes widening before she finished. Fear coursed through them when she looked at Cassidy again. "Does the captain know about this?"

Cassidy shook her head. "I doubt it. He gave me the bag, but all the envelopes were inside and so far, they have all been sealed."

Ivy bit her lip as she looked at the still mostly full bag. Then she pulled back her petite shoulders and exhaled. "Let's finish reading the rest and see if there are any more. Then, I think we need to think about showing this to him."

"I'm sure it's nothing," Cassidy began. She didn't want to make a big display out of it, especially on her first shift back.

"Maybe, but what if it's not? You can't mess around with this, Cass. This is your life we are talking about."

Ivy was right, but this was not how Cassidy had imagined returning to work. She was already on the captain's radar. This might send him over the edge, but if this stalker turned out to be real and not just threatening words on paper, it would be worse if she didn't tell him.

JORDAN RAN a hand across his stubbled chin as he stared at the run-down building. It was even worse than he'd pictured. Graffiti covered the walls and the boards over the windows. The building was brick, so the structure might at least be sound but who knew what would be waiting inside.

Jordan had spent the little time he had that afternoon trying to convince Graham to sell, but his brother had been adamant their father would have wanted them to re-open the bar. Jordan wasn't so sure. Their father hadn't even told them about this bar, much less run it the last thirty years, but then they hadn't spoken to their father much in the last few years. Not since their mother left him.

Jordan had been fifteen then and old enough to remember all the times their father yelled and hit and threw things. The broken glass, the black eyes, the lies. Graham, on the other hand, had only been ten, and either he had blocked out those moments or been so desperate for a father that he didn't care. Graham had visited their father several times when he had reached out to them and claimed he was sober, but Jordan couldn't stomach the man. How could a father do what he'd done?

With a sigh, Jordan stepped out of his car. His hand touched his side to make sure his gun was properly holstered. He went nowhere without it, and he'd worn it so long that he often felt incomplete if it wasn't strapped in its usual place.

Graham had said they would meet outside and go in together, but as Jordan was late and Graham was nowhere to be seen, he assumed his brother had started without him. Figured.

"I thought you were going to be here two hours ago." Graham's annoyed voice carried across the large room as Jordan pulled open the front door.

"Case ran long. What can I say? I'm here now." He shrugged out of his leather jacket and laid it across a table before rolling up the sleeves of his shirt. Then he placed his gun on top. His eyes scanned the room, but it was as bad as he'd expected. Old tables and chairs coated in a white layer of dust took up most of the space. The bar was a mahogany monstrosity that had probably been popular in the seventies if the orange and red colors of it were any indication. Shattered glass was all that remained of the mirror that had once stretched behind the bar. At least both of them would be going. Graham had agreed to not have a bar in the restaurant.

Graham put down his hammer and folded his arms across his chest. Fire burst from his eyes as he fixed Jordan with a fierce stare. "Are you saying my time isn't important? I had things to do this evening too, but I was here at five like we said we would be."

Jordan rolled his eyes, tired of this argument.

Graham did this every time he was late for something, and okay, Jordan was late a lot, but generally for good reason. His job as an intelligence officer in the police unit often had him working crazy hours, but he wouldn't trade it for the world. Graham on the other hand sold insurance. Predictable was his middle name, and Jordan doubted he'd had anything planned except working on his computer which appeared to be his only hobby. Sometimes Jordan wondered if they truly were related as they were so different.

"No, I'm not saying my time is more important." Though he was fairly certain it was. Graham wasn't getting criminals off the street; he was writing insurance policies and taking pictures. "I'm simply explaining why I'm late, but Graham, look around, man. This place is going to break the bank trying to fix it up. We should sell it and cut our losses."

Graham pushed his glasses up his nose and shook his head. "This is all cosmetic, Jordan. A little hard work and elbow grease will fix this place right up. As long as the walls are good, we'll have no trouble re-opening this."

Jordan bit the inside of his cheek to keep his frustration in check. He didn't want to spend his time fixing up this place. He had little free time as it was, but Graham had that gleam in his eye - the one that said he'd already made up his mind and nothing Jordan said was going to change it. Jordan supposed he could pull his big brother card and put his foot down, but Graham seemed to need this, and after years of looking out for him, Jordan still felt like he owed his little brother something to make up for his childhood. And if that meant opening a restaurant, he would find a way to make it work. "Fine, how do we tell if the walls are good?"

Graham picked the hammer back up and turned to the wall. "We remove this paneling and look inside the walls. Then we'll have a better idea of how much this renovation is going to cost."

"More than we have," Jordan said under his breath. Well, more than he had anyway. Graham made decent money selling insurance, but Jordan was paid by the city and few people got rich off a city paycheck. He grabbed the extra hammer and joined Graham at the wall. "What happens if what we find behind this paneling isn't good?" he asked as he jammed the back of the hammer into a space between panels. Images of termite eaten wood filled his mind along with the thousands of dollars it would take to fix them. "Then will you consider selling?"

"No, it will just mean it will take more money to fix it up. One way or the other, I am re-opening this place, Jordan."

Of course he was. It didn't really matter what Jordan

said. Even though Graham was younger, he had always been bossy. It was probably one reason they did so few things together. Well, that and Jordan's schedule. As a special unit detective, he was basically on call most of the time. He worked a normal shift, but it wasn't unusual for his normal shift to turn into a much longer one if they caught a lead on a case.

Jordan wedged the hammer under a crack in the paneling and heaved. The wood screamed in protest - a high pitched squeal that was unpleasant to the ears but thankfully short. With a loud crack, the wood broke in half. Jordan pulled on the broken piece until it came loose from the wall. Then he tossed it aside and ripped the top piece off as well.

Jordan wasn't sure what he had expected to find behind the paneling having never torn any off before, but it certainly wasn't the rolls of paper he saw. "What is this, Graham?" He held the roll up for his brother.

"I don't know, but I have some over here too." Graham grabbed a roll from his section of the wall and motioned for Jordan to follow him to a table.

They unrolled the tubes and Jordan stared in disbelief at the image before him. "Are these...."

"Movie posters," Graham finished. "And they look old."

Jordan gazed down at the woman in flapper attire.

"Old? These look like they're from the twenties. What was Dad doing with these?"

"Who cares? Do you know how much these are worth?" Graham asked. Excitement threaded his voice and Jordan could almost see the dollar signs in his eyes. Leave it to Graham to focus only on the money. "Come on, let's see how many there are."

Jordan followed Graham back to the wall. He hoped they might be worth enough to help with renovations, but he was still curious as to where they came from and how their alcoholic father ended up with not only a bar but rare movie posters paneled in the walls.

CHAPTER 3

*C*assidy stood outside Captain Fitzgerald's office gathering her courage. She knew she had to tell him, especially if there was any possibility that the stalker might come to the firehouse and put her or her fellow firefighters in danger, but it didn't make the conversation any easier. He was already angry she had gone on the show. Cassidy had no idea how he would react to this.

"Come in." His gruff voice carried through the closed door at her knock. Was he like this with everyone? She had always felt he didn't really like her, but unless the man was psychic, he couldn't know she was at his door. Swallowing her fear, she pulled her shoulders back and entered the office.

In addition to being fierce and laconic, Captain

Fitzgerald was a minimalist. His bookshelf sported more space than books and only one picture frame sat on his desk. Like the man himself, everything was neat and meticulous and in its proper place.

"Captain, can I have a minute?" Her voice was too quiet and what was with the tremble? Why did he have such a power over her? Was it simply because he was her boss?

His gaze flicked to hers, and his eyebrow arched on his stony face. "Marcel. I thought you'd be busy opening all your fan mail or cleaning the truck as I tasked you with doing."

Cassidy took another step in, forcing her eyes up from the worn carpet to the intimidating figure behind the desk. "I was, sir, opening the mail that is. I haven't gotten to the truck yet, but I will." Ugh, she was rambling, and her heart was thudding in her ears. She took a deep breath and tried again. "The letters are what I need to talk to you about. There were a few that stood out that I thought you should know about."

His piercing gaze fixed hers for a moment as if scanning her for a sign of weakness. Then he rolled his eyes and motioned her closer to the desk. "What is it then?"

Cassidy held out the three letters they had found that appeared to be from the same man. "The handwriting appears to be the same and the word choice looks consistent, so I'm fairly certain these are from the same guy. He seems to escalate, and while he might be harmless, I wanted to make sure you were aware of these. Just in case."

With a sigh, Captain Fitzgerald picked up the first letter and scanned it. His jaw tightened as he turned the page and his features grew stonier with each one. "Do you know this man?" he asked Cassidy when he had finished reading.

"No, sir. At least I don't think I do. I don't recognize the writing, and he didn't leave a name or a return address." Of course, she couldn't remember the last time a man had written her anything. A note, a card – it had definitely been a while.

"Wonderful, so we have no idea who or what we are looking for. You've put this firehouse in danger Marcel with your publicity stunt."

It hadn't been a publicity stunt, but Cassidy was not going to argue the point with the man. "I'm sorry, sir. That was never my intention."

"Be that as it may, you have. I'll bring this up in the next meeting and inform everyone to be on the watch for shady characters hanging around the house. As for you, if you receive anything else from this person or any unusual things start happening to you, I want you to call the police. I need your mind on the job and not on this."

"Yes, sir. I will." How she was supposed to keep her

mind completely on work with the words from the letter running through her brain she wasn't sure, but she would try.

"Good. Now, I think it's about time you got to the trucks."

"Yes, sir." Cassidy took the clear dismissal and backed out of the office. It had been bad, but not as bad as she'd expected it to be.

"What happened?" Ivy asked when Cassidy returned to the bunk room. She had cleaned up the pile of mail and cleared the beds. Cassidy wondered briefly what she had done with all the other letters but decided she didn't care. She wished she could put the whole experience behind her and just forget about it. No, she wished she had never gone on the show in the first place.

Cassidy sighed as she sank onto her bunk. "He's going to share it at the next staff meeting."

"That's it?" Ivy's eyes grew wide with concern and her fingers tugged on a lock of her hair. Either a nervous gesture or a long-ingrained habit, Ivy pulled at her split ends whenever anything bothered her.

Cassidy shrugged trying to mask the fear she felt inside. "He seemed angry but not especially concerned. Told me to watch out for anything else strange and take it to the cops if anything happened. Then he told me to get to cleaning the trucks."

"Well, if he doesn't think it's a big deal, then maybe

it isn't. He's been doing this job a long time, so he probably knows."

"Yeah, let's hope so. Anyway, I better get out there and get to cleaning." She wanted to clean about as much as she wanted to watch paint dry, but at least it would get her mind off this stalker for a while.

"Have fun with that. I'd offer to help, but I don't know the first thing about cleaning fire trucks."

"It's fine. It's actually a fairly tame penance for as mad as he was." Cassidy pushed herself off the bed and headed to the truck bay, but before she could even begin gathering the supplies to wash the truck, the alarm sounded.

"Truck 51, Squad 4, Ambulance 3, 2219 Eastside Street."

"You remember how to do this?" Bubba asked Cassidy as he hurried past her to his gear.

Cassidy shot him a withering look. "I think I can manage it." She followed him to the hooks that held their gear and pulled on hers. Donning them was like riding a bicycle, but she'd forgotten how heavy the extra equipment was. Still, she was determined not to show it. The boys needed no more ammunition with which to tease her. Hat in hand, she climbed up beside Bubba and took a deep breath to slow her racing heart. Then she closed her eyes and sent up a prayer for their safety.

"WHOA, HOT DATE LAST NIGHT?" Alayna "Al" Parker asked as Jordan set his extra-large coffee mug down on the desk across from her. Her hazel eyes twinkled mischievously above her petite nose. With perfectly clear skin and long blonde hair, Al looked more like she was eighteen than her actual age of nearly thirty which helped with stings but annoyed her the rest of the time. She got carded everywhere.

Jordan blew out an exasperated breath as he collapsed into his chair and took a swig of coffee. "I wish. My brother and I inherited an old bar and we were up most of the night tearing off paneling and assessing the damage."

Al's eyebrow shot up. "You're keeping a bar?" She knew a little about his past and his father and was obviously shocked by this news.

"No, I'm keeping an old building that *used* to be a bar. Unfortunately. We're remodeling it to be a family-friendly restaurant sans bar." He rolled his eyes and downed another swig. Even this large triple shot coffee wasn't making him feel more alive. "Graham thinks it will be great."

"And what do you think?"

He shook his head as a frustrated laugh escaped his lips. "I think it's a money suck and we should sell it. I don't have time to fix up or run a restaurant. I barely have time to buy groceries for myself."

"So, why'd you say yes? Why not just make him buy you out?"

And there was the million-dollar question. "Because he's my little brother. Because he had a crappy childhood." Jordan had told Al most of his past already, so he knew this wouldn't come as a shock to her. "I've spent half my life looking out for him and trying to make him happy. I guess I'm still doing it."

"I could help," Al said with a shrug.

"You?" Al was tough, probably more than she needed to be, but he still couldn't see her hauling out old furniture and decorating the interior.

"Yeah, I grew up with two older brothers. I learned how to swing a hammer." She leaned closer and glanced around the small room, "and though I don't do it here, I know how to use a broom."

Jordan chuckled at her persistence. Not many of his other friends would volunteer to do dirty work. "All right, I'll keep that in mind."

"Where are we on the abduction cases?" Jack Stone asked as he entered immediately shifting the energy in the room. Though Jordan was sure it was his real last name, it was ironic how well it fit him. In his mid-fifties, Jack had a full head of salt and pepper hair that he kept immaculately cut - probably an old habit from the military. His face rarely displayed any emotion and even his voice was deep and gravelly. More importantly, he was good at his job, and he didn't like to lose.

Jordan tapped his phone to make sure he hadn't missed any last-minute messages before giving his report. "I spoke with my criminal informant, but all he could tell me was that he thinks he saw a kid matching our description leave Hyder Park with a man wearing dark clothing."

"That isn't much to go on," Stone said, disappointment in his voice. "How about you?" He turned his attention to Al whose thin shoulders pulled back as she sat straighter.

"I found a camera that might have gotten footage near where we think one of the abductions happened. I was planning on going there today to see."

"Good, the two of you do that." Stone walked to the white board where all their evidence hung. Though his gaze traveled over everything, it remained the longest on the pictures of the three kids – one girl and two boys. "Albright and Givens are canvassing the neighborhoods again and doling out advice to keep kids safe, but that's only going to last so long. This guy will strike again, and we need to find him before he does."

"Yes, sir." Jordan downed the last of his coffee as he stood. No time for more. He would have to hope his adrenaline would kick in and keep him awake. Across from him, Al grabbed her jacket as well and headed for the door. He hurried to catch up with her and followed her down to the car. Generally, he preferred driving but this was her lead, and he would let her run with it.

"So, your restaurant. Are you going to let me come help?" Al threw the question out nonchalantly as she reached for her seatbelt, but Jordan sensed something deeper behind it. He'd had the feeling she was looking for more than a partnership the last month, but he wasn't interested. He didn't have time for a relationship and his mother had always impressed upon him that he should never date where he worked. Plus, his last one had gone up in flames, so he wasn't looking to jump into the fire again anytime soon.

"Yeah, maybe. It's still a mess right now."

She flashed a crooked smile at him as she turned the key and fired up the engine. "I don't mind a little mess."

Jordan knew that. While his workspace was always pristine, hers was often overflowing with papers. She called it creative genius, but he just called it a mess, and he had no idea how she found anything she was looking for. "I know you don't, but I'm not sure what the next step is. I'll definitely let you know when I have a better idea." Or not. He didn't want to do anything that might make her think he wanted more than a partnership. "So, where are we going?"

She glanced quickly at him before turning her

attention back to the road. "A convenience store over on Fifth. It's near the school where we think one of the boys was grabbed."

Jordan could tell she knew he had changed the subject on her, but it was safer this way. Dating your partner opened the door for lapses in judgment that could get you killed, and if they broke up, it would make for a very uncomfortable work environment. "Good catch. I hope they have something."

CHAPTER 4

Fatigue weighed on Cassidy as she walked to her car the next morning. Twenty-four-hour shifts were hard on their own, but add a fire into the mix and they were downright exhausting. Plus, she hadn't pulled a long shift in over a month. She hadn't thought her body would become out of sync so quickly, but it had. Normally, she would have three or four of these shifts in a row, but the captain had given her just one to let her ease back into the routine. She had the rest of the day to recoup and then she'd be back on shift tomorrow.

Cassidy opened the driver side door and threw her bag in before sliding into the seat, but as she shoved the key in the ignition, something caught her eye. Glancing up, she spied something white tucked into her windshield wipers. A ticket? But that made no sense. She was in the firehouse's parking lot and not parked in a handicapped space. A note? Ice trickled into her veins. Was it another message from the stalker?

On high alert, her eyes darted around the parking lot for any shadows or unknown strangers. Curiosity chomped at her nerves, but she wasn't going to get out of the car until she knew it was safe.

Assured there was no one else in the lot or at least not close enough to nab her in the time it would take her to grab the note, Cassidy opened her door and snatched the paper off the glass. Not wanting to take any chances, she clutched it in her hand until the car door was closed and locked again. Then she summoned her courage and unfolded the paper.

The handwritten words appeared angry and threatening on the single sheet with a definite hurried slant. Unsure if police would be able to gain much information just from the handwriting, she scanned for anything else that might be usable - an added symbol, a signature, a fingerprint smudge, but there was nothing. Nothing to give any clue who was writing this. However, the wording was consistent with the other letters - "I can show you that we belong together."

But it was the final phrase that set her heart thudding in her chest. "I don't know why you aren't responding to me, but if you don't believe me, I'll find a way to show you." The words alone held a chill but when added to the rest of the letters, the chill turned into flat out fear. And this hadn't come in the mail. It had been put on her car which meant that he'd watched her arrive yesterday when she came into shift. And if he knew what she drove, what if he followed her home? As much as she didn't want to, this was something the captain needed to know. However, as walking the parking lot no longer felt safe, Cassidy drove to as close to the front entrance as possible before hurrying out of the car and inside.

"Marcel, what is it? I thought I sent you home," Captain Fitzgerald said as she tapped on his door frame.

"You did, sir, but before I made it out of the parking lot, I found this." She held up the paper. "It's another note, and he left it on my windshield."

Captain Fitzgerald's eyes widened. Only slightly. But it was enough to increase the fear Cassidy was already feeling. If he was reacting, it meant he was worried, and if he was worried, she definitely should be.

"I'm calling Stone. It's time you told the police about this." Stone was the head of the special investigation unit. Cassidy knew little about him other than his fierce reputation implied his name fit him to a tee.

Captain Fitzgerald picked up the phone and dialed before Cassidy could speak, so she simply nodded and waited.

"Stone? It's Fitzgerald. I have a situation occurring

over here. One of my firefighters is getting threatening notes, the latest one on her windshield while here on shift. Cassidy Marcel. Yeah, the one who was on the TV show." He paused and glanced at Cassidy. "Yeah, I can do that. Thank you."

He replaced the phone in the cradle. "Stone is sending someone over. You will stay here until he arrives and you will do what he says. Is that understood?"

Cassidy opened her mouth to protest. The fierce independent part of her wanted to tell Captain Fitzgerald that she didn't need some cop telling her what to do. However, she had to admit this stalker had her on edge and a part of her was relieved to have the police involved. "Yes, sir. I will."

After leaving the office, Cassidy wandered back to the bunk room to wait for whoever Stone was sending over. She knew no one in the special investigation unit, but if they worked for him, they were bound to be good. The man had a reputation for being thorough and hard on anyone who wanted to be in his unit.

"Marcel? What are you doing back? I thought the Captain sent you home." Bubba's voice carried out of the kitchen as she passed the common room.

She didn't want to worry him, especially since he acted like a big brother, but he would be more annoyed if she didn't tell him. With a small sigh, she changed her course and entered the kitchen. "Hey, Bubba. I, um, have to wait to give a statement to one of Stone's guys."

He set the towel down he had been using to dry dishes, crossed his beefy arms, and fixed her with a penetrating gaze that said she better spill all. "Why?"

Cassidy plopped down in one of the barstools across the counter from him and sighed. Her eyes focused on the Formica counter and the light gold sparkles sprinkled throughout it. "Because someone left a threatening note on my windshield."

"And?" Bubba should have been a detective himself. He seemed to have an internal radar that knew when there was more to the story.

"And since it appears to be from the same person who was sending me stalkerish letters while I was on the show, the captain wants me to report it." Cassidy spat the words out in a rush and waited for the tongue lashing she was sure he was about to dole out.

"As he rightly should. Why didn't you tell me about this earlier?" Though his voice held no anger, there was a clear expression of disapproval on his face at being left out of the loop.

"Well, to be fair, Captain Fitzgerald said he would mention it at the next staff meeting, and then we kind of got busy with the fire." Cassidy was making excuses, and she could tell he knew it, but she couldn't tell him the real truth. She could tell him she hadn't wanted to worry him which was partly true. She could tell him she hadn't thought it was a big deal which wasn't true at all, but neither of those was the real reason. The real reason she hadn't told him was because she didn't want him looking at her the way he was now. Like she couldn't handle herself. Like she needed to be rescued. Like she wasn't a real firefighter because she was afraid of something.

That last thought was stupid and she knew it. All firefighters were afraid of something. Besides, he probably wasn't thinking any of those things, but she was a woman in a man's field. She had to be better, she had to be stronger, and she hated that she wasn't.

"You should have told me, Cass." Disappointment clouded his voice and filled his stiff posture.

"I know." She dropped her eyes to the counter again. "I'm sorry. I thought it was nothing, just some random fan, you know? But when I found the note on my car, I knew it was more serious."

"Hey." He placed a finger under her chin and tilted it up. "I know you think you have to prove yourself here, but you don't. We know how strong you are. Don't do something stupid by trying to be a hero when your family is here to support you. Always."

Tears sprung to Cassidy's eyes. He was right of course. They might tease her, but these men put their lives on the line with her every time they went into a fire together. They trusted her inside the burning heat and would support her outside of it. "I won't. I promise."

"Cassidy Marcel, you have a visitor at the front desk."

Cassidy looked up at the intercom and shrugged. "Gotta go, but I'll fill you in later."

"You better," he hollered after her.

"JORDAN, IN MY OFFICE A MOMENT."

Jordan's head snapped up at Stone's command. Al shot him a wide-eyed look that held the same question his mind did. What had he done? He shook his head to tell her he didn't know as he pushed back his chair.

"Yes, sir?" he asked as he breached the doorway.

"Come in and shut the door."

Jordan pulled the door shut behind him and then sat in one of the chairs across the desk. He shouldn't be nervous. He'd done nothing wrong, but Stone had the ability to send your heart thudding with just the tone of his voice. "What can I do for you, sir?"

"Captain Fitzgerald called. Evidently one of his firemen is receiving threatening notes. He wants someone over there to investigate it." Stone's steely gaze was meant to keep Jordan from questioning his orders, but Jordan couldn't help himself.

"But sir, I'm in the middle of this abduction case, and my CI-"

"We're all in the middle of this abduction case, but Fitzgerald is a firefighter and we look after each other. If he says he needs our help then we give our help. Is that understood?"

Jordan didn't understand why he had to go. This was probably the case of some lonely woman who'd been rescued and was now suffering from the Florence Nightingale effect. It happened to rescuers all the time. In fact, he'd had a few women express their undying love for him after particularly dangerous cases. Why couldn't Stone send Al or one of the other less senior members? But it wasn't his place to question. Stone was in charge. "Yes, sir. I'll go check it out."

"Good. She's waiting at the firehouse for you."

"She?"

Stone's brow arched as he regarded Jordan. "Yes, she. It's Cassidy Marcel."

Jordan stifled a groan. "The one who was on the reality dating show?" He never watched it, but Al did and when she found out someone from their city was on it, she had regaled him with a recap of every episode.

"That's the one. You have a problem with that?"

"It's just," Jordan ran a hand across his stubbled chin, "it's probably just some lonely guy who is looking for a little fame. Wouldn't I be more useful here working on finding these kids?"

"Would you feel that way if it were your mother or your sister or your girlfriend?"

Jordan stifled a sigh. He still didn't want to spend time dealing with a stalker, but Stone was right. If this had happened to a woman in his life, he would want the best person possible looking into the case and protecting her. "Fine. Point taken. I'll head over there now."

Stone nodded and turned his attention to his computer. The discussion was clearly over, and Jordan took his cue and left the office.

"Where are you going?" Al asked as he grabbed his jacket off the back of his chair.

"To the firehouse. I'm sure I'll be back soon."

"You want me to come along?"

"No, I've got this. Keep looking for more footage. I want to get this guy before we lose any more kids."

Twenty minutes later, he pulled into the firehouse parking lot. His eyes scanned the lot as he parked, but other than the car blocking the entrance, nothing seemed out of the ordinary. Was that an employee's car? Or had the stalking escalated? There'd been no call over the radio, so surely there wasn't a hostage situation, but then why was the car parked like that? It was a clear fire hazard.

He checked his gun as he stepped out of his car, but

it was safely strapped to his side and nothing gave him cause to pull it as he crossed the parking lot to the front door. Unsure what he had expected, he was still taken aback by the door opening to a small atrium with a reception desk.

"Can I help you?" the woman occupying the desk asked.

"I'm Detective Jordan Graves to see Cassidy Marcel." He flashed his badge to assure her of his identity as he rarely wore a uniform. His work required him to blend in, not stand out.

The woman gave a perfunctory nod and picked up the phone. "Cassidy Marcel, you have a visitor at the front desk." She replaced the phone and motioned him to the few chairs in the room. "She'll be here in a minute. You may sit if you'd like."

Jordan preferred to stand. It was easier to be ready should anything happen, but he didn't have to wait long anyway.

"I'm Cassidy." A woman with long brown hair pulled back in a ponytail which accentuated her broad shoulders and slender neck approached him. She wasn't quite what he'd expected as little makeup graced her face though it was peppered with miniature freckles. She had the air of an athlete rather than the prima donna he'd imagined. A few papers were clutched tightly in one hand, but she extended the other to him in greeting.

"Detective Jordan Graves." He shook her outstretched hand wondering why she had gone on a reality dating show. Low self-esteem? A bet? Or was she one of those girls who looked low maintenance but demanded constant attention? He knew that type well. His last girlfriend had been one.

"Shall we go somewhere quiet so I can fill you in?" she asked. Her voice was soft and sweet and not at all like the princess-type voice he had expected.

At his nod, she led the way down the hall and into a conference room. When the door was closed behind them, he pulled out a chair and sat down. Might as well jump right in. The faster he finished here, the sooner he could get back to finding missing kids. "Okay, so tell me what's going on."

Cassidy sat across from him and straightened the papers before placing her hands on them. She took a deep breath as if summoning the courage to speak. "Yesterday was my first day back on shift. I took some time off to do a show."

"A reality dating show. I'm aware." He hoped she hurried this up because he wanted to get back to his investigation.

A pink flush crawled across her cheeks. "Yeah, a dating show. Anyway, when I arrived yesterday, I had a bag of fan mail. Captain Fitzgerald made me go through it and when I did, I found a few letters that gave me pause." She pushed the first few pieces of paper across the table to him.

Jordan picked the first one up by the corner and scanned the contents.

Dear Cassidy,

I'm enjoying watching you on the show, but you deserve better than Tyler. In fact, I think we would be perfect together.

The writer was clearly enamored with Cassidy but other than stating he felt they belonged together, there wasn't anything sinister in it. He set that page aside and read the next letter.

Dear Cassidy,

Tyler wouldn't know a good woman if she were given to him on a platter. I know how to treat a woman better, and I would love the chance to show you.

More of the same but still nothing to get upset about. He hoped she hadn't called him here just for these. Jordan glanced at Cassidy as he put that page aside as well, but her intense expression didn't give the impression she was simply seeking attention.

He turned his attention to the third letter, and his eyes widened slightly.

Dear Cassidy,

I don't know what you see in Tyler. I would treat you so much better and I'll prove it when you return from the show.

"Did you receive any letters on set from his guy?"

Cassidy shook her head as her bottom lip folded in

under her teeth. "I don't even know who this guy is. While I was on the show, I had no contact with anyone, and I had no knowledge of who was watching. I didn't even know I was getting fan mail until I walked in the door yesterday morning."

He raised a brow at her but said nothing. She might not have known about it, but she probably enjoyed it. After all, who went on a reality dating show if they weren't looking for attention? "Is there anyone in your life who paid you extra attention before you went on the show? Anyone who gave you pause?"

Cassidy pursed her lips as she thought. "There's a guy who's a little odd in my apartment complex. He's always walking his dog and he tries to strike up a conversation whenever I'm around, but he seems harmless. Besides, wouldn't he just leave notes on my door if it were him?"

"Maybe, but if he's tried to get your attention that way and failed, he might try something like this. What's his name?"

"Dustin, I think." She dropped her eyes to the table as if embarrassed. "He told me once, but to be honest, I didn't pay much attention."

Jordan nodded. That didn't surprise him, but he couldn't fault her as he was guilty of the same thing. He knew there were women who'd talked to him whom he hadn't been interested in and had dismissed. It was something he was working on, but he certainly hadn't mastered it yet. "That's understandable. How about ex-boyfriends or men you turned down?"

A flush of pink spread across her cheeks. "I haven't had an ex-boyfriend in some time, and he left me so I'm not sure why he'd stalk me. There have been a few men who asked me out after I saved them from a fire, but I always said no and never heard anything else from them."

He wondered what her story was. She was pretty, not model beautiful, but attractive in her own way, and she appeared confident in her own skin – a quality a lot of women he had dated seemed to be missing. Maybe, like him, she was just too focused on her career right now, but then why go on a reality dating show in the first place?

"Do you remember any of their names?"

"My ex, sure, but the rest," she shook her head sadly, "I don't. I never really knew them in the first place."

Great. That didn't give him much to work with. "Well, the letters don't sound like your ex. They're worded differently, not like someone who knows you personally. Unfortunately, that doesn't help us narrow it down much. I'd say just keep your eyes open and be aware of your surroundings."

"There's more," Cassidy said. "Today, when I left, I found this on my windshield." She slid the final piece of paper to him. "I don't know how he expected me to respond since he never left a name or a return address."

He picked it up and scanned the writing.

Cassidy,

I know you're back in town, and now I can show you that we belong together. I don't know why you're not responding to me, but we will be together whether you know it or not. We belong together, and I'll find a way to show you. I'll be in touch soon.

Okay, maybe he was being too hard on her. He doubted this was the kind of attention she had been seeking. The guy was escalating, and he could see why Captain Fitzgerald would want her to report it. "You say this was on your windshield?"

She nodded and her right hand lifted to tug at her earlobe. Nervous gesture? He had seen few people display that particular gesture, but she didn't wear earrings, so a nervous gesture made the most sense.

"He must be someone you've had contact with before, but it could have been any contact. Often stalkers build a relationship in their head over little things, so he might be someone you met in a store or helped at a fire. He thinks you had a connection, so he believes he's given you enough clues to know who he is. This note on your car means he was probably hanging around when you arrived. Do you remember seeing anything out of the ordinary?"

Another tug as her eyes darted to the side. "No, but I

wasn't looking for anything. It was my first day back on shift. I was just glad to be here." She dropped her hand from her ear and folded it into the other one before fixing him with her dark brown eyes. They were rich and deep, the color of dark chocolate, and they held the tiniest hint of vulnerability. "What do I do?"

Jordan cleared his throat and focused his attention on the papers. He had no business reading anything in her eyes. He was too busy on his current case for anything else. "Unfortunately, there still isn't much we can do at this point. I'll take this in for processing, but I doubt they'll find anything. They're short for one thing, and while handwriting can tell us about a person, there isn't a database of handwriting to compare this with like there is with fingerprints. Do you have the envelopes they came in? Was there a return address?"

As a wince crossed her features, he knew before she spoke that she no longer had them. "No, no return address, but I think Ivy threw the envelopes away. I didn't think we'd need them."

Of course she hadn't. "Who's Ivy?"

"One of our paramedics and my friend. She helped me open the envelopes. There were a lot of them."

He glanced up at her. Was she bragging? Maybe his first impression of her being a diva had been right. "Okay, I'll follow up with her to see if we can get those envelopes back. There might be DNA if he licked them.

In the meantime, I'll escort you home. He may already know where you live, but if not, perhaps a police tail will discourage him from following. I'll check out your place before you enter to make sure it's clear, and then I'll sit on your block for the next hour."

He reached into his pocket and pulled out one of his cards. They didn't hand them out often, but the simple card contained his name and cell number so that CIs or people like Cassidy could get a hold of him quickly. "If you see anything after that time, you call this number, and I'll be there. If something happens, we'll get a police detail on you until we catch this guy. Any questions?"

Cassidy turned the card over in her hands before flashing another disarming, crooked smile his direction. "I probably have so many, but I don't even know what to ask right now."

Jordan nodded and pushed back his chair. "That's understandable." Careful to touch the papers as little as possible, he folded them and tucked them in the Ziplock bag he pulled from his pocket. "I doubt we'll find anything on these, but I'll have the lab run it for prints anyway. Did anyone else touch it?"

Cassidy blinked at him. "Um, Captain Fitzgerald might have when I first showed it to him and Ivy touched the first few but not the one on the windshield."

"Okay, I'll get prints from all of you so we can rule them out, but let's get you home first."

Her eyes shifted to the side again and when they returned to his gaze, they held just the slightest hint of fear. "What if he follows us back and learns where I live?"

Diva or not, his heart went out to her. He knew what it was like to live in fear – he'd done it for the first fifteen years of his life, and while it made him who he was today, he wouldn't wish it on anyone. That helpless feeling was hard to ignore.

Jordan didn't want to tell her that if the guy had staked out her job and figured out her car, he probably already knew where she lived or how to find out anyway. "That's what I'm there for. The police presence should deter him, and I'll keep a watchful eye out as we drive. Don't worry. I'm good at spotting a tail."

With a determined set to her posture, she pushed back from the table, took a deep breath, and nodded. "Okay then. Let's go."

CHAPTER 5

*C*assidy felt a little safer as she walked to her car with Jordan behind her. He didn't advertise it, but she knew he carried a gun strapped to his side. She was no stranger to firearms having grown up with older brothers who taught her how to handle one, but she didn't have a concealed carry license. Perhaps she should look into getting one and brushing up on her training. Her experience was pretty limited to shooting coke cans off the trash barrel in their backyard growing up.

"Let me check your car first," he said as she pulled out her key fob.

She held it out to him and watched as he popped her hood and then her trunk. She hoped he didn't look in the backseat as she hadn't had time to clean it out since her return.

Cassidy had a tendency to be on the go so much that it almost appeared she "lived out of her car." Though she had a trash bag, wrappers and cups generally landed on the floorboards instead, and she'd lost count of how many items she had left in the car - coats, books, even her phone on occasion, so needless to say, it wasn't the neatest car on the block. And Jordan was handsome. His blue eyes stood out under his dark hair like blazing beacons, and the muscular tone of his biceps beneath his shirt sleeves had not gone unnoticed. She didn't want him thinking her a slob as well as a diva.

He hadn't called her that, but she had seen the look in his eyes. It was hard to miss since she'd received it from nearly everyone since returning. That look that assumed she had gone on the show for fame and wondered when she would flit off to the next opportunity.

She couldn't blame them, really. The same thought had popped into her mind when she first considered going on the show, but it wasn't why she had gone. And though she could tell them her real reason had been looking for love, it seemed silly now since she had come home empty handed. It was easier to let them assume.

Jordan dropped to the pavement and scanned under the car, then slid into the driver seat. After inserting the key, he paused as if listening for something. Then he turned the key. When the engine fired up, he exited the car.

"All clear. My car's just over there. Don't leave the lot until I'm right behind you. Then I want you to make sure you can always see me in your rearview mirror. Do you understand?"

Cassidy nodded though she wasn't sure if his words were easing her fears or ramping them up.

"If we get separated, pull into the closest lighted parking lot and wait for me. You have my number, so you can call and tell me where you are. I doubt that will happen, but if it does, do not get out of your car."

Yep, definitely ramping the fear up. Her heart thundered in her chest, but she was determined to appear calm. "I understand."

He waited until she was in her seat with the doors locked before sprinting to his car. After a similar check of his own, he fired up his engine, and she headed for the exit.

Even though she knew he was watching, Cassidy found herself peering out of the windows and checking the rearview mirror religiously. She saw nothing out of the ordinary - only his headlights, but there was still a part of her that worried this guy would follow and try something once Jordan was gone.

No lights were on in her apartment when she pulled

into the parking space, but could he be hiding in the dark waiting to stab her? Or worse? She didn't want to think about all the things that could fall under 'or worse' but they filled her head anyway. Her heart fluttered faster in her chest.

She wasn't usually one to jump at shadows but this was such an unknown territory for her. As she'd told Jordan, there had been a few men who tried to hit on her at fires or the few times she had gone with Ivy to the hospital to check on patients, but none had ever gone farther than asking her out. They'd all taken her polite decline and turned their attentions elsewhere.

She opened her door to step out, but before she could shut her door, Jordan was at her side. His hand raked across his stubbled chin as his eyes scanned the area. "Let me go in first and check the place out. What number is it?"

"It's apartment A, straight ahead," she said pointing.

He followed her finger and then turned back to her. "Do you have a separate house key from your car key?"

"No, but I can take it off the ring." As she released the house key from her ring, her mind shifted to her house. Had she put everything away? The house was still a little messy from her whirlwind unpacking, but she thought she had at least put her undergarments in her dresser. And even if she hadn't, knowing she was safe was more important than worrying about him seeing her underwear.

"Stay in the car with the doors locked until I return. If you see or hear anything suspicious, drive to the police station and ask Stone to send help."

The fluttering in her heart increased. "Do you think he's in there?"

Jordan shook his head, but his gaze lingered only briefly on her as his eyes darted around the parking lot again. "I don't. I didn't see a tail, but it's always better to be safe than sorry in my line of work."

Cassidy swallowed trying to ease the fear gnawing in her stomach. "Okay, thank you." Then she climbed into her car and locked the doors.

JORDAN WAITED until he heard Cassidy's door lock before continuing up the small walkway to her front door. He stilled his breath and listened as he inserted the key, but silence was all he heard. As the door swung open, he pulled his flashlight from his pocket and his gun from his holster. He preferred to search with lights on, but as he didn't know where all the switches were, this would do until he could find them.

The door opened to a simple living room. In the low

light, he could make out a chair, a couch, and a small end table. He swung the light to the left and the right flicking on the light switch when he spied it. Nothing moved as the light dispelled the shadows, but Jordan took another moment to verify the surroundings before continuing into the house.

The room extended into a kitchen and a single hallway led away from the living room. Probably to the bedrooms and bathrooms, but he would need to check the kitchen first. From where he stood, almost all of it was visible, but a center island blocked some of his view and the rest of the kitchen resided behind a wall. Not a ton of places to hide but enough, and kitchens contained knives. He didn't want to be blindsided by a maniac wielding a knife.

Cautiously, he stepped forward keeping his ears hyper-aware for any sounds. The small kitchen held no surprises other than a cluttered counter. How many appliances did one woman need? A toaster, a waffle maker, a blender, and a coffee grinder filled her counters. Did she use them all every morning?

Focus! He needed to focus. He was securing the house not dissecting the woman though she seemed like she might be an interesting one to dissect. He moved out of the kitchen and down the hallway. Three doors. All closed. He hated closed doors as they made it harder to get the upper hand on someone. With a deft twist, he turned the knob and pushed the door open, pointing his light and gun in at the same time, but this door held only a small closet. Stuffed to the brim with coats and shoes but nothing else.

The next door opened into a bathroom. Again, he was struck by the sheer amount of clutter on her counter. Bottles of product, a brush, and at least two hair appliances filled the small space. Maybe she was a diva type after all. Or was this a common trait for most women? His fiancé had also kept a ridiculous amount of beauty products in her bathroom, but then she had turned out to be a diva.... or at least not the woman he had thought he was marrying.

The last door must lead to the bedroom then and it was cracked. Had she left it that way or was someone inside? He heard no sound from inside, no shuffle, no rifling, no drawers opening and closing, so if someone was in there, they were either still or possessed ninja-like skills. With a swift push, he opened the door and crouched, but nothing flew at him.

After flicking the light switch on, he cleared her bedroom. While no one was inside, he'd have to ask her if she'd left it this way because it looked as if a tornado had touched down. Clothes hung out of overstuffed drawers and littered the bed. A half-packed suitcase sat in the corner begging to be emptied. How she could live like this was beyond him. His place was spotless, but perhaps some of that compulsiveness came from being a cop.

He slid his flashlight into his pocket but kept his gun out as he walked out of the house and back to Cassidy. She opened the door and stood when she saw him approaching, and he could read the questions in her eyes. Man, her eyes were like a mirror reflecting her inner emotions. He wondered if she knew how easy she was to read.

"All clear. There's no one inside, but it looks like your bedroom might have been tossed."

Cassidy's cheeks flamed as she dropped her eyes to the pavement. Her toe twisted a small half circle on the concrete. "No, that was me. I just got back from the show and haven't unpacked fully. It's not usually that messy."

Jordan held up a hand to stop her. He didn't care about her mess or her excuses. He wanted to finish this job and get back to finding the missing kids. "Make sure you lock all the doors when you get inside if they aren't already. The windows too. I'll sit down the street for the next hour. After that, call me if you need anything."

"Okay, thank you, Detective Graves. I know you must have better things to do than stake out my house."

"You can call me Jordan, and it's fine," he said

cutting her off and shifting his eyes from her thankful gaze. "Just part of the job." But he did have better things to do. While he was sitting here watching for a stalker who probably wouldn't appear, another kid might disappear. Or worse.

CHAPTER 6

*C*assidy rubbed her eyes and tried to wake up, but the heaviness of sleep enveloped her like a suit of armor. She'd been too wound up to fall asleep, jumping at every shadow and every settling creak of the apartment even though nothing had been there. There'd been no phone call, no more threatening notes, but that hadn't eased her anxiety. And when an hour had passed and she knew Jordan was gone, it had only gotten worse.

At some point she must have fallen asleep as evidenced by her wrinkled clothes and dry mouth, but it certainly hadn't been quality sleep. She rubbed her eyes again. The light stung them, and her lids felt glued together. She would need a strong cup of coffee today in order to function.

With half-closed lids, she stumbled to the shower

hoping the hot water would wake her up. Going into work tired was never a good idea, but for a firefighter it could spell disaster. She needed to have all her senses working in case there was a fire.

The water managed to clear some of the haze, and the two cups of coffee after finished the transformation so that by the time she had to leave for work, she felt a little jittery but fully awake.

Her eyes scanned the area as she opened her front door. She might not be a detective, but she could look for things out of place. Nothing appeared amiss though as she walked the few feet to her car.

"Hey, Cassidy."

She jumped at the masculine voice that came from behind her and nearly dropped her keys. "Hey, Dustin." Cassidy hoped that was his name as she turned around to find him leaning against the corner of her building, his dog beside him. If he was her stalker and she said his name wrong, would he get angry and attack her? More importantly, what was he doing at her building? She thought he lived a few doors down.

"I haven't seen you around for a while. Have you been busy with work?" He stared at her evenly as he waited for her to answer.

He didn't know she'd been on the show? She supposed that wasn't entirely surprising as she hadn't advertised it, but Ivy had been checking her apartment a few times a week. Had he not noticed her? She chose her words carefully, hoping to sound nonchalant. "Yeah, life has been busy, but that's the way it is sometimes, right?"

"I suppose, but I seem to have a lot of free time. Maybe we can hang out sometime when you have some?"

Not on his life. Or hers. But she couldn't say that out loud. Not until she was sure he wasn't her stalker. "Yeah, maybe. I can't right now though because I have to get to work. Don't want to be late." Before he could say anything else, she ducked into her car. As he watched her back up and turn toward the exit, she tossed him a wave hoping the fear she felt wasn't written all over her face.

"Everything okay, Marcel?" Bubba asked as she pulled open the front door of the firehouse twenty minutes later. He lounged against the reception desk with a cup of coffee in hand as if he'd been waiting for her, and he probably had. She'd probably find him around every corner until this stalker was caught.

"Everything is fine, Bubba. Nothing new to report." Although that wasn't entirely true, she didn't have any real indication that Dustin was the stalker. "No new notes if that's what you're worried about." She smiled and gave him a reassuring pat on the arm as she passed him.

"Sleep okay?" he pushed as he fell into step beside her.

Cassidy stopped and turned to face him. "Why do you ask?"

He pointed just below her eyes. "Just wondered if those dark circles were a fashion statement or something else."

She batted his hand away. "Fine. I didn't sleep well. It was a little hard to relax worrying that some crazy guy might try to break in."

"You could stay with me until this blows over if you'd like."

His words warmed her heart. She had known her friends were amazing, but she still hadn't expected this. "Thank you, Bubba, but I'm not going to give this guy the satisfaction of turning my life upside down. Besides, who knows how long it will be before they catch him. Jordan gave me his number to call if anything happened, so I'll be fine."

"Jordan, huh?" She didn't miss the teasing lilt in his voice.

Cassidy opened her mouth to tell him it wasn't like that – there was nothing romantic going on between her and Jordan er Officer Graves, but before she could, the alarm sounded.

"Truck 51, Squad 4, Ambulance 3. Fire in the Huntington Apartments. 412 Merriweather Lane."

Cassidy hurried to the bunk room to drop her stuff

and then joined the others at the engine and quickly donned her gear.

"You awake enough for this?" Bubba teased as he grabbed his hat and stepped onto the rig.

Cassidy wasn't sure. The coffee was still coursing through her veins, but she didn't feel herself and didn't like it.

"Man, I hate apartment fires," Luca said as the truck roared out of the firehouse.

"Only because you hate stairs," Deacon pointed out. "If you ate a little better, you wouldn't hate them so much."

Luca turned his fiery gaze on Deacon. "I could take you any day, Jackson."

"Okay, let's focus on what matters here," Captain Fitzgerald said.

The men quieted and Cassidy reached up to touch the small silver cross that hung around her neck. It wasn't flashy, but knowing what it symbolized always seemed to calm her spirit. She sent a silent prayer up as the truck swung into the parking lot. Apartment fires were dangerous because there were multiple floors and they could give out at any moment. The possibility of falling to your death or being crushed when a floor caved in loomed in her mind.

"All right, it looks like the fire is on floor two. Marcel and Campbell, you take that level. Go door to door as quickly as possible and get the stragglers out. Sanders and Jackson, you clear the lower level. Witherspoon and Kalhoun, you take the third floor. Let's get everyone out alive, hear me?"

"Yes, sir," they shouted in unison before pulling on their masks and filing out of the truck. Cassidy followed Bubba into the main entrance. Her mother had once asked her how she could run into a burning building, but Cassidy rarely thought about it. It was her job, so she did it, but today the mask felt stuffier, the fire hotter.

Bubba motioned her to a back staircase that looked solid and intact and they made their way up it. The second floor was full of smoke which seemed to be coming from the apartment farthest away.

"Let's go quickly," Bubba said, the mask distorting his voice.

"Fire Department," they called out as they headed down the hall.

Cassidy pushed open the door on her right and entered the apartment. "Fire Department, call out." Her voice sounded muffled behind the SBCA mask. She cleared the main room and then headed down the short hallway. "Fire Department. Anyone here?" The sound of crackling flames filled her head, but there was no other sound. The bathroom and bedroom were empty as well.

"Anything?" Bubba asked when they met again in the hallway.

Cassidy shook her head. "I'll check the next one, but we better get some retardant on the last apartment before we lose it entirely."

"Our job is just to clear it. Let's finish up and report back to the captain."

With a nod, Cassidy pushed against the next door, but it didn't open as the others had. She stepped back and threw her shoulder against the door. It moved barely an inch, but it was enough to see that a body was blocking it.

"Bubba! Bubba, I need you," Cassidy yelled as she pushed against the door again. Moments later, she heard Bubba's footsteps behind her and with his force, the door moved enough. "Grab her and get her out," Cassidy said. "I'll make sure there's no one else."

Bubba glanced up at the fire. "Don't be long. We don't have much time."

"Just get her out of here." Cassidy continued into the apartment as Bubba pulled the woman out. "Fire Department, call out." Only the roar of the fire answered her. Sweat rolled down her spine from the pressing heat, but she continued through the apartment. The rest of it was empty as was the hallway this time when Cassidy re-entered and continued to the last apartment.

The unbearable heat pushed against her, but she had to be sure. She pushed against the door and nearly fell back from the wave of smoke and flames that roared out to meet her.

Cassidy pushed against the invisible wall of heat and called out. Flames licked up the walls and sweat rolled into her eyes sending a burning sensation that set her blinking. She turned to head toward the bedrooms but something on the floor caught her eye. A doll? Was there a child in here? Her head swiveled to the right and the left, but there didn't seem to be anything else indicating a child. No highchair, no gates, no other toys, but the couch appeared out of place. Cassidy crawled behind it expecting to find a child huddled there. Instead, she found a hole in the wall. What in the world?

Ignoring the encroaching flame, she crawled closer to the hole. Two leather straps hung from the wall and a bowl like a dog dish sat in the middle of the floor. What was this? A cage?

"Marcel, it's time to go."

Cassidy stood to see Witherspoon and Kalhoun standing in the doorway with the hose.

"There might be a kid. I haven't gotten to check the bedroom or bathroom yet."

"Captain said it's time. We'll keep our eyes open for a kid."

Cassidy cast another glance at the hole in the wall.

She should obey the order, especially since she was on thin ice with Fitzgerald as it was, but something didn't feel right here. "I think it's a girl. Please."

"We've got this," Witherspoon said and motioned for her to get out of the way so they could fire the hose.

As they headed past her to cut off the flame, she grabbed the doll and exited the apartment. She had questions, and she was going to get answers.

"How was your babysitting gig last night?" Al asked with a smirk as Jordan sat down across from her.

"Who told you?" He certainly hadn't. After leaving Cassidy's, he'd stopped by the restaurant and helped Graham clear out the broken mirror. Graham had sent the movie posters to a collector and secured a sizable sum from them which thankfully was going to pay for most of the renovations, but there was still a lot of work to do.

"Stone," she said with a shrug. "I asked him where you were, and he said you were checking out a stalker for Cassidy Marcel."

"Yeah, one she acquired while she was on that show you love so much, but it was a waste of time. Probably just some random fan. Anything new on the case?" He turned on his computer and waited for it to load.

"Not yet. I mean on one hand that's good news. No new kids taken that we know of, but we still have no idea where they are or how to get to them. Stone is getting anxious."

Jordan was getting anxious too. It didn't usually take them this long to nab whoever they were after, but this guy was slick. It was like he was a chameleon, changing every time so their intel was never good.

His phone vibrated in his pocket and he pulled it out expecting to see the number of his CI, but it was an unknown cell number. "Graves," he said holding the phone to his ear.

"Jordan? It's Cassidy."

Jordan stifled a groan. He couldn't deal with more stalker nonsense today. "Hey, Cassidy. Did you get more notes?"

"What?" Her voice held a note of confusion. "No, this isn't about the stalker. I need to know if you can investigate a scene."

Jordan's brow furrowed. Firefighters didn't usually call cops to investigate a scene. "I'm a little busy with a kidnapping case."

"I wouldn't have called if it wasn't important. I took it to Captain Fitzgerald first but he dismissed my concerns."

Jordan wondered if he should be doing the same thing, but there was a sense of urgency in her voice that gave him pause. "Okay, why do you want me to investigate a fire scene? What's going on?"

There was an intake of breath and then, "About an hour ago, we returned from an apartment fire. In one of the apartments, Bubba and I found an unconscious woman. He pulled her out and I continued to secure the apartment. That apartment was empty and I didn't find anyone else in the last apartment, but I found a doll."

So far Jordan was not seeing the sense of urgency or the need to call him. "Okay, so what? Maybe the people who lived there got out." Or didn't, but he didn't want to say that out loud.

"That's the thing though. There was nothing else in the apartment that suggested a child. No other toys, and there's one more thing." She paused for a moment and Jordan tried not to rush her. "As I was leaving, I saw the couch looked out of place. I thought a child might be behind it, but I found a hole in the wall instead."

Suddenly Jordan sat up a little straighter. A hole in the wall was odd but combined with the out of place doll, it felt a lot more suspicious. "Did you look in the hole?"

"Yeah, there were two leather straps as if someone had been tied up in there and a blue bowl like a dog dish. Captain Fitzgerald doesn't believe me that there might be something criminal happening there, so I thought I would take a chance and call you. I know you're busy and you don't know me, but -"

"Are you still at the fire house?" he asked interrupting her.

"Yeah, I'm on shift until tomorrow morning."

"Okay, tell me where the fire was and we'll go check it out." Jordan's gut was rarely wrong and right now it was telling him this might be worth looking into. He wrote down the address Cassidy gave him and hung up the phone after promising to call her with any information.

"Come on," he said to Al. "We need to go check out a fire."

"A fire?" Confusion colored her expression. "Isn't that a firefighter's job?"

"Yeah, it's something she said she saw at the fire."

Al's eyebrow lifted. "She? You mean the one you babysat last night? Do you even know anything about her? Maybe this is just an attention getting stunt."

Jordan stared at Al. She wasn't usually one to pass judgment before getting to know someone, and he wondered if her attitude was jealousy of Cassidy's air time or the time she had spent with him. "Maybe it is, but what if it's not? What if there's another missing kid out there somewhere and we don't investigate it?"

Al rolled her eyes and sighed, but she grabbed her jacket. "Fine, we'll go check it out."

Though it was clear Al thought Jordan had lost his mind, she followed him to the car, and he filled her in on the way to the apartment complex.

"Are you sure it's safe to be here?" Al asked as they stepped over the yellow caution tape and entered the charred building. "Shouldn't we make sure the structure won't collapse before we walk about?"

Al was right. They should have someone with them who could verify the building could sustain their weight, but his intuition was telling him there was no time to waste. "We have to see if Cassidy was right before someone comes back and destroys the evidence."

"Okay, but you're going first."

The main floor appeared rather untouched by the fire but Jordan had no idea what the second floor would hold. When they came to the staircase, he placed his foot gingerly on each step waiting for it to fall out from beneath him. Only when it held, did he continue to the next step.

The second floor was definitely in worse shape. Remains of wall paper curled off the walls looking a little like eerie fingers reaching out to them and the smell of smoke still hung heavy in the air. Cassidy had said it was the apartment farthest back, so he headed that way hoping the floor would remain solid.

The door to the apartment hung off one hinge and a sea of black swam before them. This had to be where the fire started as it appeared to be the area most badly damaged. He scanned the room as they entered looking for any sign of children that Cassidy might have missed, but she was right. There was nothing. To his left, he saw the remains of a piece of furniture that must have been the couch.

"Do you want to tell me what we're looking for?" Al asked as she stepped lightly across the floor.

"Cassidy said there was a hole in the wall behind the couch and she thinks maybe someone was tied up in it. Someone small." He let the words hang in the air. "Like a child."

Recognition flickered in Al's eyes as she hurried to his side. "You don't think the guy we're looking for lived here, do you?"

"I think it's worth investigating." He stepped behind the couch hoping to see the hole that Cassidy had. The leather straps might have burned in the fire but maybe they could get DNA off the dish. All his hopes, however, were dashed when he saw the wall. The fire had burned the wall behind the couch completely. There were no straps.

"Do you think she was wrong?" Al asked as she surveyed the scene.

Jordan shook his head as he crouched down. He didn't know Cassidy well. It could be that she had an attention-seeking disorder and this was just another effort to fuel her ego, but then why become a firefighter? Yes, it got you attention, but it could also get you killed.

He pulled his gun from his holster and used the barrel to move the ashes around. Not knowing what else might be in the mess, he didn't want to take the chance of using his bare hand, but when his gun uncovered a hardened blue puddle, he forsook caution and grabbed the item.

"What does that look like to you?" he asked as he held the melted plastic up.

Al's nose scrunched in disgust. "A mess. What are you doing touching it?"

"It looks to me like the color of a dog dish, you know the plastic kind you buy at the store." Okay, so that was a bit of a leap, but he couldn't think of anything else that would be in the walls and look like this.

"So, she was right." Al's words were soft, breathy.

"It appears she was. Now, the question is… who lived here?"

CHAPTER 7

"Okay, thanks for letting me know." Cassidy hung up the phone and sat down on the couch.

"Was that Jordan?" Bubba looked away from the TV which was playing the latest football game and wiggled his eyebrow at her. He was the only guy in the firehouse she had confided in before going on the show, and sometimes she wished she hadn't. Now, he seemed determined to make any guy she met a possible love interest.

Cassidy rolled her eyes to let him know how far off base he was although she couldn't deny she found Jordan attractive. She definitely hadn't missed how well his jeans fit his frame when he was crawling under her car or how sexy he looked with his gun drawn as he entered her apartment. "Yes, but it's not what you think. I asked him to check out the apartment from the fire earlier. He couldn't find the hole in the wall because the fire damaged it too much, but he did find a lump of melted plastic he thinks might have been the bowl."

Bubba let out a low whistle and turned his full attention to her. "So, what's the next step?"

"Jordan is checking with the landlord to see who rented the apartment, but I think that will be a dead end. I'm going to check with Ivy to see if I can talk to the woman we rescued. She might be our only hope in finding this guy." Cassidy picked up the blackened doll she had taken from the apartment and sighed. "And this kid."

"She was pretty beat up and had a lot of smoke inhalation. It may be a few days before she can talk."

"I know. I just hope it gives us enough time."

"Marcel, isn't it about time to wash the truck?" Captain Fitzgerald's voice carried in from behind them.

"Yes, sir, I was just about to do that." Cassidy stood and tucked the doll behind her back. She'd tried to talk to the captain when they first returned from the fire, but he'd dismissed her concerns. He probably thought she was trying to get out of the work he'd placed on her, and though that wasn't the case, she hadn't wanted to argue with him.

"I'll talk to you later," she whispered at Bubba before ducking out of the room. She dropped the doll off on her bunk before heading to the bay. Some little girl was missing that doll, and Cassidy was determined to return it to her.

As she entered the bay, she hit the button to open the doors. At least it was a nice, warm day. She hated washing the truck when it was cold outside.

"Oh, hello, I was just about to knock, but I wasn't sure where the front door was."

Cassidy glanced up to see a man standing just outside the bay doors. He was nice looking in the nerdy Clark Kent way with dark hair, glasses, and a suit.

"Sorry, my car won't start, and I was hoping someone here might have jumper cables. I'm pretty sure it's time for a new battery but just haven't had time you know?" He shrugged and pushed the glasses up the bridge of his nose.

Cassidy sized the guy up. Normally, she would have thought nothing of a request like this. After all, the firehouse was nestled in a housing development, so visitors showed up often, but the ominous notes were still on her mind and going anywhere alone with a stranger, even one that looked like he couldn't harm a fly, didn't seem smart. Plus, the guy seemed vaguely familiar though she couldn't place where she'd seen him before.

"Actually, we have something even better. Just let me grab it and let them know where I'm going." She flashed him a small smile. "I'm supposed to be washing the truck."

"Sure, of course, thank you."

Cassidy stepped back inside and hastened to the common room where Bubba still sat watching the game. Luca and Deacon had joined him and all three were glued to the screen.

"Aren't you supposed to be washing the truck, Marcel?" Luca asked.

"Yes, and I'm going to start in a minute, but there's a guy who needs a jump. I just wanted to let someone know where I'd be." She emphasized the last few words hoping Bubba would catch her drift.

He glanced up and nodded letting her know he had her back and would come to check on her in a few minutes. It wasn't quite the reaction she had hoped for, but at least it was something.

She grabbed the battery jumper on her way back to the bay. "Okay, all set. Where's your car?"

"Just over here." The man led the way out of the parking lot and to the right. "Thank you so much. I'm supposed to be on my way to a meeting, and I thought I was going to be late."

"Well, this does take about ten minutes to charge the battery. I hope that gives you enough time."

He checked his watch which appeared to be a Rolex – the man had money or at least wanted to appear like he did. "It'll be tight, but I think I can make it. I'm glad it was you I saw first."

Cassidy froze as fear washed over her. "I'm sorry?"

"Oh, you probably don't remember. You checked the carbon monoxide levels at my friend Brian's house a month or so ago. I never got your name then, but I wanted to thank you. I had no idea you worked at this station. I'm Scott by the way." He held out a smooth hand.

Cassidy looked at it, not sure she wanted to shake it but even less sure she wanted to decline and risk angering him. She remembered this call. A nice house with a group of men watching a football game. One had complained of migraines and an odd smell, so they'd called in the fire department to make sure there was no carbon monoxide leak. It had been a routine call, and the men had all seemed nice and stable. She needed to get ahold of herself. The guy needed a jump. That was it. He'd given no indication of anything else. She was letting her fears control her. "Cassidy," she said finally shaking his. "This plugs into your cigarette lighter. You do have one, don't you?"

"Oh yes, it's not that new. It's this one." He unlocked the door of an older Ford Mustang and held the door open for her. "I probably should upgrade especially with this battery issue, but I just love older Mustangs, don't you?"

"Yeah, I guess." Cassidy wasn't much of a car girl. As long as it drove, it was good enough for her. "Here, you just plug this in and push the button." She handed him the device and stepped back. Her fear was probably unfounded, but harmless or not, she'd seen enough movies to know he could slam her with the door and cause some serious damage. Images of Kathy Bates from the old Misery movie flashed through her mind.

He plugged the charger into the port and flicked the power button before backing out of the car. "So, now we wait?"

"Yep, now we wait." The silence settled between them – heavy and uncomfortable. "So, what do you do?" She didn't need to know his occupation nor did she care, but small talk seemed less awkward than staring at each other in silence for ten minutes. However, she didn't want to let her guard down and give this guy a chance to overpower her if he did have nefarious intentions, so she leaned against the back door careful to keep a comfortable distance between them without drawing attention.

"I'm a financial planner. I set up IRAs and things like that. Boring but necessary." He flashed her a crooked smile and Cassidy returned it, mostly out of habit, but he did have a nice smile and it eased her trepidation a little. "How did you get into firefighting?"

Cassidy hesitated. Should she tell him? It wasn't

anything too revealing and she couldn't see the harm in sharing. At least it would help pass the time. "On a bet actually."

Scott's eyes widened behind his glasses revealing eyes the color of a stormy sea. They were the most interesting color Cassidy had ever seen. "Really?"

"Yeah. I was in college and not sure what I wanted to do. There was this guy on my hockey team who thought women were inferior to men in every way, so he told me I couldn't make it through the firefighter academy. Not one to let him win, I had to try, and I fell in love with it. Switched my major to fire science, graduated, and here I am."

Scott shook his head and grinned. "Well, remind me never to bet you anything. I have a feeling you rarely lose."

Cassidy's smile faltered. Yes, she rarely lost, but she hadn't always won, and the sting of the one she lost still left its mark. That had been her last boyfriend, David. She'd spied him in a crowded restaurant, and after her friend dared her to ask him out, she had sidled up to his table. He'd been flattered and agreed, and their relationship had progressed quickly. To the point where she'd thought he would propose. She'd already planned the entire day in her head and the kids they would have after. Then, one day, he'd up and left. Said her job took up too much of her time and his secretary held his interest more.

"Have you had a fire today?" he asked glancing toward the firehouse.

"What?" Cassidy shook her head to clear the painful memory from the past. "Yeah, we had one this morning. A fire at an apartment complex."

"Oh, dear. I hope no one was hurt."

Something in his tone bothered Cassidy though she couldn't place her finger on what. She glanced at her watch. The charger still needed another few minutes. "I don't think so, but I was only on one floor, and our paramedics handle injuries more than we do."

Scott nodded and glanced at the firehouse again. "Well, it sounds very exciting anyway. I bet it keeps you busy."

Cassidy watched his gaze slide to her left hand. Was he searching for a ring? Was this guy her stalker after all? How much had she shared? Too much? Suddenly, her heart began to pound in her chest. He'd made no move toward her, but if he did, could she run fast enough? Could she overpower him? She hated this feeling, this fear that every man she met might be out to harm her. Would she face this the rest of her life?

"Yep, a firefighter's life is busy. Pretty much work and sleep."

"That's too bad," he said holding her gaze. Could he see her fear? "There's more to life than work and sleep."

From inside the car, she heard the timer ding, and a feeling of relief washed over her. "Looks like you're all done. Why don't you try to start the car?"

Cassidy took a step back as Scott stepped toward her and then leaned into the car. The engine fired to life and he smiled at her. "What do you know? Thank you for your help."

"Sure. If you could just pull that machine out, I can put it back and you can be on your way." Cassidy tried to keep her tone even.

Scott leaned back into the car and then held out the starter machine. "Here you go. It was nice to meet you again. You're a lifesaver."

"It's what I do," Cassidy said with a forced smile. She took the machine and stepped back again, putting more distance between herself and Scott, but she didn't move any farther until he got in the car and drove away. Only then, did her breathing return to normal and her heartbeat begin to slow. She had to find out who her stalker was. There was no way she could keep living like this.

"Dang it," Jordan hissed in frustration as the computer

came up empty again. He'd gotten the name of the renter from the landlord who'd confirmed he had rented to a single man, but so far that name had done nothing for the case.

"No luck?" Al asked.

"None. Whoever rented that apartment is a ghost. There's a million Michael Simmons, but no one with the matching social the landlord gave us, and the social is actually registered to a guy who died five years ago."

"Were there any cameras in the apartment?" Stone asked as he paced the room like a caged tiger. The movement raised the tension in the room which was already thick. The kids had been gone too long and they all knew the statistics, but none of them were willing to give up.

"No, it was too old," Al supplied. "None across the street either."

"Do we have anything else to go on?" The frustration created a hard edge in Stone's voice.

"There might have been a witness. Cassidy said they dragged one woman from the scene. I'm waiting to hear from her."

"Let's hope she knows something," Stone said as he scraped his knuckles across his stubbled cheeks. Usually clean shaven, the scruff accentuated his stress. "I feel like the trail is going cold and I don't like that. Not ever, but especially not when kids are involved." The slam of his office door punctuated his agitation.

"Cassidy, huh? Is there something going on between you two?" Al made the words sound innocent, but Jordan could tell from the sideways glance she shot him that there was more than idle curiosity behind the question.

"Not like that. She's a part of the case, that's all." But was that all? He couldn't deny there was something attractive about Cassidy, but no, the last woman he had opened his heart to had left him at the altar. He wasn't going to go down that path again any time soon.

"Okay, if you say so. Hey, you want to grab some dinner?" Al's abrupt shift took Jordan by surprise and he blinked at her a moment before he could form words.

"I can't," he said with a sigh. "I promised Graham I would help with the restaurant tonight. He wants to clear out all the old furniture and the monstrosity of a bar so we can start looking at interior designs." Although Jordan knew with Graham in charge there would be much less decision making and more informing of what the choice would be.

"So, how about we grab a pizza and I'll help. Broom, remember?" She wiggled her eyebrows and flashed a wide smile.

Jordan wanted to say no. He didn't want to lead her on, but having someone be a buffer with Graham might be nice. "Okay, but don't say I didn't warn you. The place is a mess."

"I'll consider myself officially warned. Come on, I'm starving." Al grabbed her jacket and headed for the door. Jordan had no choice but to follow.

After a quick stop at a local pizzeria, Jordan parked in front of the old building. The windows were still boarded up as Graham had suggested they fix the inside before the outside, so as not to attract vandals or thieves.

"Looks lovely," Al said in a teasing tone as she opened her door.

"Yeah, well, I told you. The inside is worse." He opened the door for her as she carried the pizza box.

"Late again, I see…." Graham's voice trailed off as he spied Al behind Jordan.

"Sorry, but we brought food. Graham, this is my partner Al. Al, this is Graham." Jordan took the box from Al as he made the introductions in case she wanted to shake hands.

"This is your partner?" Surprise and just a hint of disbelief filled Graham's voice.

Al leaned back and crossed her arms. "Is that a problem?"

Jordan squeezed his lips together and watched the scene unfold. Al's defensive posture was up and when she felt threatened, or in this case slighted, she was like a cornered raccoon who could claw your eyes out before you expected it.

Graham must have sensed it as well because he stumbled over his next words. "No, it's just he never mentioned you were a woman. With the name Al, I assumed…"

"Al is short for Alayna, and that's what you get for assuming."

Jordan chuckled as Graham's mouth fell open. Al might be small and look young – in fact, she had posed as an underage girl in more than one sting – but she was tough as nails and not afraid to speak her mind.

"I… I'm sorry." Graham stuttered over the apology trying to recover.

"It's cool. I guess Jordan doesn't talk about me that much." This time she turned her penetrating eyes on him.

With a shrug, Jordan brushed her accusation off. "To be fair, I don't tell Graham much about work. Now, I thought you said you were starving. How about we eat?"

"Yes, let's eat." Graham's face told Jordan that he would have questions to answer later, but right now he was glad to be out of the hot seat.

CHAPTER 8

*C*assidy grabbed her bag and headed for the door. Though there were showers and beds in the firehouse, nothing replaced the feel of her own pillow-topped bed, and after three days on shift, she was ready to be home and curl up in her own bed.

"Cass, wait up."

Cassidy turned to see Ivy hurrying her direction. Her pixie face sported a mischievous smile. "Hey, I met the nicest doctor at the hospital today. Tall, dark, and handsome. I think he'd be perfect for you and he's free tonight."

Cassidy tried not to roll her eyes as she sighed. She knew Ivy meant well, but her bruised ego was still healing from Tyler's rejection, and set up dates were usually worse than regular ones. Friends always meant well, but the added pressure just made the dates even more uncomfortable. "Not tonight, Ivy. I've been on shift for three days. I want a real shower and decent sleep in my own bed."

"Okay, but soon, right? You need to get Tyler out of your head and start dating again."

"I will. I promise. Just not tonight."

Ivy crossed her arms and narrowed her eyes at Cassidy. "All right, but I'm holding you to that promise."

Cassidy had no doubt she would. The girl was tenacious like a dog who wouldn't give up a bone. It was one reason she loved her. Most days. "I'll see you in a few days, Ivy."

The air was cool as Cassidy stepped outside the firehouse, and the last of the sun's rays stretched across the parking lot. Twilight was her favorite time of day as the colors reminded her of a fire, but a peaceful one.

"Hey, I was hoping I would see you again. I was just about to knock."

Cassidy jumped at the voice and clutched her bag tighter, her body tensing as it decided whether to fight or flee. To her right, a man stepped out of the shadows. The Clark Kent whose car she had jumpstarted.

"Sorry, I didn't mean to scare you. I wanted to bring you these as a thank you." He held out a beautiful bouquet of flowers as he stepped closer. "Thanks to you, I didn't miss my meeting."

"Oh, you didn't have to do that." Cassidy took a step back. He had to be her stalker. Why else would he have shown up again so soon? She ran through her options. There was a small can of mace in her bag, but she'd never get it out in time. She could throw her bag at him in distraction, but she doubted she could make it to her car before he caught her. Screaming was an option, but would they hear her inside the firehouse?

"I know I didn't have to, but it was an important meeting. Thanks to you I didn't lose the client. I was hoping maybe I could take you to dinner."

Dinner? There was little doubt in Cassidy's mind now. What would he do if she said no? Would he go crazy and attack her? He didn't look as if was carrying a gun or a knife, but that could be part of his ruse — look normal and unassuming to lure women into a sense of safety and then turn on them and take them down before they could run.

Cassidy wished she had a panic button on her phone that would alert someone, but there was no way she could make a move without arousing his suspicion. "I just got off shift and am pretty tired," she began, but she didn't get to finish because Ivy burst out of the front door excited and out of breath.

"Cassidy. The woman from the fire..." Her voice trailed off as she caught sight of Scott. "Oh, sorry I didn't know you had company."

Ivy wasn't Bubba or Deacon or even Luca and she certainly couldn't take this guy down, but at least there was safety in numbers. "Ivy, this is Scott. I helped him jump his car the other day and he was just stopping by to say thank you."

"And to ask you to dinner," he piped up.

Ivy's eyes widened as she looked from Scott to Cassidy. "Right, well, I'm sorry to interrupt." She stepped back as if she were going to re-enter the firehouse, but Cassidy wasn't about to let her do that.

"No, it's fine. I really have to go anyway, but why don't we exchange numbers and get in touch soon." Cassidy had no intention of giving him her real number, but she hoped she might get his. Maybe Jordan could run it through some system and let her know if he was legit or dangerous.

"Uh, sure." He pulled out his cell phone and tapped a few buttons. "Okay, go ahead."

Cassidy rattled off a number close to her own hoping Ivy wouldn't rat her out and then put his number in her contacts.

"At least take these," he said handing her the flowers, "and thank you again."

When he was out of earshot, Ivy tugged on her arm. "Do you think he's the stalker?"

Cassidy shook her head though she wished she knew. She didn't like thinking the worst about someone she didn't even know. She'd worked hard after David dumped her to focus on seeing everyone as God did instead of seeing them through the burning hatred she felt for David. "My guess is yes. He comes out of nowhere asking for a jump and then shows up with flowers and a dinner invite?"

"Or he could just be a nice guy who is attracted to you," Ivy said playing the Devil's advocate, "but he probably won't be when he tries your number and finds out you gave him the wrong one."

Cassidy watched the car pull out of the lot and resisted the urge to shiver. "Just seems too coincidental to me. Plus, he gave me the creeps the day I helped him. He asked a lot of questions and stared at me."

"All things guys do when they're interested in you," Ivy said. "Maybe it has been too long."

"It didn't feel like interest," Cassidy said with another shake of her head, "but look, I'll see if Jordan can find anything out on him. If he's not my stalker, I have his number and can contact him and explain."

"If he listens long enough to hear your explanation."

Frustration exploded inside Cassidy, and she turned on her friend. "Whose side are you on anyway?"

An expression of hurt clouded Ivy's face. "Yours, of course, I just hate seeing you like this. You're scared, I get it, but not every new man you meet is your stalker. There are good guys out there, you know?"

"So, you keep telling me." Cassidy looked down at the bouquet of flowers in her hand. She hadn't wanted them in the first place, but after this conversation, the mere sight of them brought a sour taste to her mouth. "Here, enjoy these." She shoved them in Ivy's hands knowing she would have to apologize later but unable to deal with it right now. "I've got to call Jordan and get to the hospital."

Before Ivy could protest, Cassidy hurried to her car and started the engine. As she drove out of the lot, she dialed Jordan's number. "Jordan? Meet me at the hospital. Our woman is awake."

JORDAN FOUND Cassidy waiting at the nurse's station for him. "She's able to talk? Does she remember anything?"

Cassidy chuckled and shook her head sending her dark hair swishing against her shoulder. She wore it down today, and it looked like chocolate silk. "I don't know. I waited for you before going to see her. Ivy asked them to call her when she woke up and she told me right before I called you."

"Okay, well, let's go see if she can help us." Jordan followed Cassidy down the hall to room 108 trying to keep his focus on the case and not the woman in front of him which was becoming harder with each moment he spent with her. They knocked quietly on the door before pushing it open.

A frail looking woman lay on the bed. Burns covered her face and arms, but though burns weren't his expertise, Jordan thought she'd been lucky. They didn't look like third degree burns.

"Ma'am?" Cassidy's voice was soft beside him.

The woman opened her eyes and stared at them. "Who are you?" she asked in a hoarse whisper.

"My name is Cassidy and this is Jordan. I was one of the firefighters who rescued you from the fire, and Jordan is a police officer."

Jordan stepped closer to the bed. "We need to ask you some questions about the fire. Did you know the man in 2D?"

"I can't say that I knew him, but I saw him a few times when his mail would get delivered to my apartment − 2B."

"Did you ever see him with a child?" Cassidy asked. "A girl maybe?"

The woman appeared to think for a minute. "No, I never saw a child, but I suppose there could have been one living there. The mail I got had at least three different names on it. I just figured he was scamming the welfare system especially when I asked him about it and he told me to mind my business, but I suppose it could have been mail for other people who were living there. Never saw any others though."

Other names? Could they be lucky enough that he would have used his real name on one of them? "Do you remember the names?" Jordan pressed trying to keep his tone even.

"No, but I had just gotten some mail for him that day. I was on my way to give it to him when I realized I had forgotten a few other pieces that were sitting on my table. Before I could go back to get them though, something hit my head and the next thing I knew, I woke up here."

"Do you think the pieces would still be there? On your table?" These names would help them. Jordan was just sure of it.

"If the fire didn't get them. You're welcome to go in my apartment and look." She turned her eyes to Cassidy. "I didn't even know there was a fire. Do you know if my apartment was damaged?"

"Most of the fire was in his apartment. You might have smoke damage though. If you want, I can come back after we grab the letters and let you know."

Tears filled the woman's eyes. "Thank you. I don't have much, but a lot has sentimental value, you know?"

Cassidy nodded as if she understood, and Jordan realized she most likely did. Dealing with fires every day, she probably saw this reaction quite often from people.

"Thank you, ma'am," Jordan said as he stepped back. "You've been extremely helpful."

Cassidy followed him out of the room and fell into step beside him. "So, are we going back to the apartment?"

"We?" he asked. "No, I am going back to the apartment. You are going back to work or home or wherever you need to go."

Her jaw tightened and she pulled on his arm with a grip that was surprisingly strong and halted his step. "This is my case too. I'm the one who found the doll and the hole and called you." She ticked the items off on her fingers for emphasis. "I want to see this through."

Jordan thought about fighting her, but something flickered in her eyes. A defiant spark, and somehow, he knew she wouldn't take no for an answer. "Fine, you can come with me to the apartment, but then your job is done. The rest is on me, got it?"

She narrowed her eyes at him as if debating whether to push it further, but in the end, she agreed.

"Let's take my car there. No sense in taking two," he offered as they exited the hospital.

"Fine with me."

Jordan watched Cassidy as she climbed into the car and buckled her seatbelt. He'd assumed she was a diva when he first met her, but now he was seeing a whole new side of her. One that intrigued him but scared him as well. Especially because in small ways, she reminded him of Jasmine. That sense of confidence had been what drew him to Jasmine in the first place, but it had also been what tore them apart.

Now, here was Cassidy inserting herself into his life without even meaning to but making an impression nonetheless. However, he needed to keep those emotions locked down. He didn't need romance right now and certainly not with someone who ran head first into danger. No, if he ever dated again, he needed someone with a quiet job who was content to avoid danger. Someone he wouldn't have to constantly worry about and who could be content being married to a cop. A woman who was a firefighter was about as far from that as you could get.

The parking lot of the apartment was still deserted when they arrived. "I guess it will be awhile before they re-open this," he said as he turned the engine off.

"If they ever do," Cassidy said. "Fires like this often destroy the structure and then it's not safe to just apply cosmetics and go on like nothing happened."

"So, where are all these people living?" Jordan glanced up at the building as they approached the yellow caution tape and pictured all the people who must be displaced right now. Having rarely investigated a fire scene, he had never thought about the aftermath for those who might live there.

"Who knows? Hotels probably or with relatives. Sometimes they never recover and take to living on the streets. Those are the hardest ones to watch." She ducked under the tape as he held it up for her.

"I can imagine. You still like it though? Firefighting, I mean."

A crooked smile played across her face as he pulled open the door. "Yeah. I like helping people. Isn't that why you became a cop?"

"Uh, not really." Jordan debated telling her a story. One that didn't involve his troubled past, but he didn't want to lie to Cassidy. "I became a cop because my dad was an alcoholic who used to beat my mom. When she finally got the courage to take us and leave, I swore I would join law enforcement so I could stop men like my father in the future."

Cassidy's face folded in compassion. "I'm sorry to hear that. That must have been rough."

Jordan shrugged and turned away. "We all have our scars." He shouldn't have told her because now she was looking at him the same way everyone did who knew. With pity. He hated that look and decided to change the topic to get the attention off of himself. "What about you? Why did you become a firefighter?"

"A bet," Cassidy said with a chuckle as she followed him up the stairs. "You may not have figured this out about me yet, but I don't like being told I can't do something."

He snickered to himself; he had certainly picked up on that trait of hers. "I bet you were a handful for your parents."

A delightful laugh escaped her lips. "I was. My mother said I used to stick my tongue out at her with my lips pursed together. Said she could tell by my eyes."

Jordan tried to picture Cassidy as a young girl. Had she been a tomboy or more of a girly girl?

"Anyway," she continued jolting him out of his imagination and back into the present, "I dated a guy in college who told me I couldn't, so I decided to prove him wrong and fell in love with it."

And there was that hint of Jasmine again. Not so much what Cassidy said, but the way she said it. As if it was the most natural thing in the world. Jasmine had been confident like that. So confident in fact that she had even convinced herself she could be a cop's wife until the day of the wedding hit, and she'd realized she wanted more. More security, more time, more something that he evidently couldn't give. Was that why he had stopped dating confident women?

"Here it is, 2B. Let's hope her apartment wasn't too badly damaged." Jordan pushed the past from his mind as he opened the door to the apartment and stepped in. There was some charring from the heat on the walls and the items closest to them, but thankfully the fire had been stopped before it destroyed this apartment.

The only issue was the woman who lived here was a clutter freak, not quite hoarder level, but papers lay everywhere as if they had fluttered down from the sky like snowflakes. "She said the table, right?" Jordan asked.

A look of disgust crossed Cassidy's face as she nodded and took a step toward the kitchen table. Papers covered it completely acting as a makeshift tablecloth. "How did she eat in here?"

"Maybe she cleaned it off with each meal?" Though he doubted it from the look of the apartment. The place didn't look like it had seen a broom or a vacuum for quite some time.

"That seems like a lot of work." Cassidy picked up a piece of paper with her fingertips. Some orange stain covered it. "Or maybe she just ate on top of them." With a shudder, she dropped the paper to the floor. "I wish I had brought gloves."

Jordan did too. He had no idea what might be in all these papers and while he wasn't squeamish, the thought of a roach crawling across his bare hand sent a shudder down his spine. "Just be careful and look for anything with a male name on it."

"Like this?" Cassidy held up an envelope. "Isn't Jeremy Irons an actor?"

Jordan took it and read the name chuckling as he

did. "Yep, I'd say our woman in the hospital was probably not named Jeremy nor a famous British actor." He set that one to the side and kept digging through the papers. "Here's another. Robert Bedford."

Cassidy gaped at him, her mouth hanging open. "*That* didn't raise any red flags?"

"I've seen a lot of weird names in my work," Jordan said. "People probably figure nothing's off the table anymore."

"What's the weirdest name you've ever come across?" Cassidy asked as she rifled through the pile on her side of the table.

Jordan thought for a moment. He'd met quite a few people who had the same first and last name – John A John or Charles Charles, but then he remembered the woman from the previous summer and smiled. "It doesn't sound weird if you say it, so I'll spell it. The name was spelled ABCDE."

The space between Cassidy's eyes furrowed as she set down her paper to look at him. "ABCDE? As a first name? How was it pronounced?"

Jordan chuckled as he remembered the lively woman. She'd been a handful. Dressed in bright colors and absolutely adamant she had done nothing wrong; she had tried to reason with Al and himself for five minutes before they managed to get her in the back of the car. "Absidee. Still an interesting name but not nearly as strange as the spelling."

Cassidy shook her head. "And I thought my name was weird. Growing up, I could never find it on those keychains or other trinkets that you buy at tourist shops. Not like my brothers who are named Wes and Paul. Pretty easy to find those, but the closest we could ever get was Cathy, which sounded similar but wasn't my name."

Jordan nodded as if he understood, but he'd never been on a vacation. At least not when he was young. When his parents had been together, his father either had drunk the money away or been too drunk to care about taking them somewhere. And after his mother left, she'd been too busy working two jobs to afford a "frivolous" vacation, but he could relate to how important a name was. Too many times, he'd wished his father would use his name instead of calling him boy. "How did you end up with the name Cassidy anyway? I mean it's pretty but definitely unique."

"My dad was a big Butch Cassidy fan, and I guess my mother vetoed naming either son Butch, but she liked that Cassidy was different." She shrugged. "So, there you go."

"Well, I think it's nice to have a unique name. I thought Jordan was like that until I went to school. Then one year I was in a class with three other Jordans. One boy and two girls."

A wide smile formed on Cassidy's face. "Yeah, I don't have that issue. Never met a boy with my name though I'm sure there might be some."

Jordan returned the smile and marveled at the ease of talking with Cassidy. She was not at all the diva he had first assumed she was and now he was even more curious why she had gone on the show. "Can I ask you something?"

Her eyes met his and he saw just the slightest hesitation in them. "Sure."

"Why did you go on the dating show? You seem so grounded and I can't imagine you enjoying all the hoopla."

"I didn't enjoy the hoopla, and I'm not, you know?"

"Not what?" Jordan asked confused. Had he missed something?

"I'm not a diva, and I didn't go on the show for fame."

His mouth fell open as he struggled to formulate an answer, "I didn't…"

"No, you didn't, but I could see it in your eyes. I didn't go for fame. In fact, I didn't want to go at all at first. When my mother suggested it, I thought she was crazy, but I've wanted to start a family for a while now, and though I dated, I wasn't meeting the kind of man I wanted to marry. So, I prayed about it and started to feel like God was leading me in that direction. That must have been my own ego though because it certainly didn't turn out in my favor."

"Maybe God wanted you on the show for another reason. One you haven't discovered yet." As he held her gaze, he realized he was suggesting that maybe she had gone on the show so they would meet. He should rephrase, explain himself. He didn't need Cassidy thinking he was attracted to her even though he was. Dating just wasn't in his future and definitely not with a woman who reminded him so much of Jasmine.

She held his gaze and electricity crackled between them. Her eyes had turned from a mirror reflecting her feelings to a microscope discerning his. Oh no, he was in so much trouble. He needed to fix this now. "I'm sorry I meant…"

She dropped her eyes to the table breaking the connection. "Edward Long."

He blinked at her sure he had misunderstood and unsure how the topic had shifted so quickly. "What?"

She held up an envelope. "It's addressed to Edward Long."

Edward Long? Why did that name sound familiar to him? He ran through the evidence he could remember from the case. His memory was good, and there was something just under the surface, but he couldn't place it.

"That's three aliases. Do you think there are any

more?" Cassidy's nose scrunched sending cute, tiny wrinkles across the bridge as she surveyed the piles. Cute? No, he didn't need to be putting the word cute with her at all. He needed to rein his emotions in.

"I think we have to be sure. It shouldn't take us much longer."

"Okay, but then can we celebrate by grabbing a burger after? I'm starving."

Was she asking him out on a date? Though he wanted to say yes, dating Cassidy would be a bad idea. "I'm not sure that's a good idea."

"Oh, come on, Detective Graves, surely you have to eat?" The twinkle in her eyes matched the teasing lilt in her voice.

He should say no. He should tell her they would never work. She was too similar to the one woman who had managed to charm and then destroy his heart, but he was hungry. And he did need to eat. And he appreciated a woman who could enjoy a good burger. "All right. I do know a great burger place just down the road, but it's not a date." Maybe if he said it enough times, he could convince her as well as himself.

She held her hands up in surrender. "Got it. Not a date. To be honest, I think I'm avoiding dating for a while what with Tyler and now the stalker."

Right, the stalker. He still hadn't followed up with that. "Have there been any more notes?"

A cloud passed over Cassidy's face momentarily. "No. No more notes but something odd I was going to ask you about. The other day, a guy showed up at the firehouse needing a jump. It's not that unusual since we're in a neighborhood but there was something that seemed off about him. Then he showed up again today with flowers to thank me and a dinner invite. It just seemed…" her nose scrunched again as if debating the word she wanted to choose, "pushy, and I didn't get a warm fuzzy feeling from him. Do you think he could be the stalker?"

A need to protect her welled up within Jordan. If this guy was the stalker, he was getting brave showing up at her job and engaging with her, which could mean he was escalating. That being said, he didn't want to alarm her any further. "It's possible. I'd like to investigate him. Do you think you could describe him just in case?"

"I could, and I got his name and number. Well, his first name anyway."

She gave this guy her number? Was she intentionally stoking the fire?

"Don't worry," she continued as if reading his mind, "I gave him a fake number in return, but is there some database you can run his number through to see if he's a liar or something?"

A soft laugh spilled out of his lips at the thought. "Well, there's no database for that, but I can see if he has a record and if he's using his real name." Had he misread her attraction? Would she date this flower guy if he turned out not to be the stalker? Whether she would or not, this was just another sign that he didn't need to be pursuing Cassidy.

"All done over here."

He looked down at his pile and realized he was finished as well. "Let's go get that burger then." He knew he was probably playing with fire, but right now, he didn't care.

CHAPTER 9

"This is your favorite burger spot?" Cassidy asked as they walked up to the open window of the burger truck. She hadn't expected an upscale restaurant but perhaps a sit-down place where they could talk. Nothing was around this truck except one picnic bench. Not even a table. They would have to hold the burgers in their laps.

"Don't knock it until you try it. These are the best burgers in Fire Beach. I'm surprised you haven't been here before." He approached the open window and quickly surveyed the short menu. "Do you trust me to order for you?"

Did she? Cassidy generally despised men ordering for her, but maybe that was because they never seemed to know her and always ordered something she wouldn't like. Somehow, even though she didn't know him well, she thought Jordan might have an idea what she would like, and if he didn't, then she would learn something about him too. "Sure, surprise me."

"Two peppered bacon burgers, two drinks, and a side of onion rings," Jordan said to the man in the open window.

Onion rings? How could he know she loved onion rings? Unless he did too. She'd felt a camaraderie with him both at the hospital and then again at the apartment. No, camaraderie wasn't the right word. She had felt an attraction growing between them even though he seemed determined to deny it for whatever reason. She wondered why. Was it his job? Hers? Maybe he couldn't date her because he was working her case. Or maybe he was going off her declaration that she didn't plan on dating? Why had she said that?

She shouldn't care what his reason was. Her heart was still healing after the interaction with Tyler, and a cop was not the kind of man she wanted to marry. Her schedule was already crazy, and though she might have to retire from firefighting if and when she became a mother, she wanted to be with someone who had a more stable schedule. Someone who wouldn't miss ball games and dance recitals. Someone who would be at church with her every Sunday. She couldn't see Jordan being that kind of guy, but that didn't diminish the attraction she felt.

"Here you go," he said breaking into her daydream and handing her a drink. Darn it, her daydreaming had distracted her and now he'd paid for the food. Did that make this a date after all? Should she offer to pay for her half?

"Could you grab some napkins?" he asked indicating the stash near the window with his head. His hands were a little full with the bag of food and his drink. "There's not much seating here, but there's a park just around the corner if you don't mind walking a little."

"A walk sounds good," she said with a smile as she fell into step beside him. She'd let the money slide for now. The evening air was cool as the sun began to set sending brilliant rays of yellow, orange, and red across the sky, but Cassidy's light jacket kept her warm enough.

A small park appeared before them, and though it held little more than a slide, a swing set, and a volleyball net, it did have a picnic table. Jordan waited for her to sit before sitting across from her.

"How did you find this place?" Cassidy asked as she scanned the park and began to unwrap her burger.

Jordan's eyes glazed over as he looked out toward the playground. "I used to bring my brother here to escape from life. When my dad started yelling, my mom would usher us out of the house. Partly to keep us safe and partly so we didn't know how much of a beating she was taking. This park was far enough away that we couldn't hear them and Graham enjoyed playing at it."

Cassidy placed a hand on Jordan's arm. "I'm so sorry. That's not the way a father should be."

"Don't I know it," he said with a derisive snort, "but it made me who I am today, and I think I'm a pretty good detective because of it."

While Cassidy knew that hard times and tragedies formed people, she wished stories like Jordan's didn't exist. She had been lucky. While her father worked a little too much when she was young, he was still there almost every night for her brothers and her, and forty years later, her parents were still married – not something most of the people she knew could claim.

"I think you're an amazing detective." She enjoyed the slight hint of pink that brushed his cheeks as she held his gaze.

Suddenly, his eyes widened and he slapped the table. "Edward Long."

"What?" Cassidy looked around expecting to see someone approaching them, but there was nothing but the approaching darkness.

"The name Edward Long sounded familiar to me when you said it, but I couldn't figure out why. But it was a name we were looking into on the case, and I interviewed him. I can't believe I didn't realize…. Would you mind taking the burger to go?"

Cassidy wrapped up her burger and tossed him a smile. "Nope. If it means you catch this guy, then I'm all for it." She had hoped to spend more time with him, but if there was a child in danger, their time could wait.

"Great." He had already tucked his burger back in the bag and was pulling out his cell phone. "Al? Do me a favor. Look up Edward Long and get me the address. I think he might be our guy."

He looked up at Cassidy. "Can you write an address down for me?"

Cassidy looked around but she had no pen and no paper. What she did have was her phone. She quickly opened the notepad app and hovered her finger over the face as she waited expectantly.

"I'm with Cassidy." He rolled his eyes. "It's not like that. We just came from the apartment fire. Al, we'll talk about this later. Just give me the address. 452 Wheeler Avenue. Thanks."

Cassidy typed the address into her phone as he rattled it off and suppressed the urge to ask him about the odd conversation, especially since it seemed his partner didn't approve of her. She didn't think she'd even met his partner, but now did not seem the time to stir the pot.

"Let's go. I'll drop you off on my way." He was

already two steps ahead of her, his toned legs taking long strides. She hurried to catch up with him.

"Take me with you."

He stopped long enough to shake his head. "No, it's too dangerous. I don't know what this guy is capable of."

"But you said you interviewed him already. He knows you and probably won't let you in without a warrant. Do you have a warrant?" Cassidy hoped she was right. She watched a lot of the Law and Order type shows with the rest of the guys at the house, but she certainly wasn't versed in the law.

Jordan's eyes shifted as he ran a hand across his chin, and Cassidy knew she had him. "No, I don't have a warrant. Okay, what are you thinking?"

"Let's run back to the station. I'll grab my gear and show up as a firefighter. Tell him there was a gas leak reported and I just need to check his apartment. You can be waiting outside."

"I don't like it," Jordan said with a slow shake of his head. "You aren't trained for operations like this. If something happened to you…"

Cassidy placed a hand on his arm trying to ignore the emotions that ignited within her at the simple touch. "It won't, but Jordan, we can't let the guy get away."

He looked down at her hand and then back into her eyes. "Fine, but we do it exactly as I say. You understand?"

"You bet."

JORDAN STILL COULDN'T BELIEVE she had talked him into this. It was dangerous and if anything went wrong, Stone would have his head. However, Cassidy was right. This guy was sly and this might be their only chance to catch him.

"Okay, just like we went over, do you understand? You walk the place pretending to check for carbon monoxide and look for any signs of the kid. If you see anything or he appears jumpy, you use the code word."

Cassidy issued a swift nod before turning those eyes on him. Though fear flickered in them, determination overshadowed the fear and Jordan's respect for her grew a little more. She was out of her element and about to do something potentially dangerous, but her shoulders were pulled back in resolution.

"I'll be in that doorframe," he said pointing to one down the hall, "until he lets you in. Then I'll move to be right outside the door, but you'll still have to speak up."

"Okay, let's do this." She adjusted her helmet and then faced the door. Her bulky uniform made her appear larger, but Jordan was very aware of how unprotected she was. He sent up a prayer for her safety and his own as he ducked into the doorway.

A moment later, he heard the sharp rap of her knuckles and then her words, "Fire Department, open up," in a clear commanding tone.

"Yeah, what do you want?" Jordan could tell from the clarity of the voice that the man had opened the door. He wanted to look to see if it was indeed the man he had interviewed earlier, but he didn't want to chance being seen.

"Sorry, sir, I need to check your apartment. There's been a carbon monoxide leak reported in the building and we need to clear all the apartments." Jordan marveled at how firm her voice sounded. If she was scared, she wasn't showing it.

"I'm busy."

"It will just take a minute, sir, but you have to let me in. Carbon monoxide can be deadly if you breathe it too long."

"Fine, but hurry up. I've got things to do."

Jordan heard the swish of her pants and knew she had entered the apartment. Now, the only question was whether Edward Long would close the door or not. He forced himself to count to ten just in case the man chanced a glance down the hallway and then he peeked around the doorframe. A sliver of light escaped from the doorway. He had left it ajar.

Careful to keep his footsteps as quiet as possible, Jordan moved down the hallway until he was outside the door. The conversation inside was muffled, but thankfully he could still hear it.

"Have you experienced any headaches, sir?"

"No."

"Is there anyone else here in the apartment with you?"

"Why does that matter?"

Jordan's breath caught at the harsh tone of the man's voice. Cassidy had better lay off the questions.

"I just wanted to make sure no one was having headaches, sir. The first sign of carbon monoxide poisoning is generally a headache, then vomiting, then dizziness. Most people pass out, but if it gets to that point, it usually means brain damage or death."

She was good and Jordan breathed a little easier when Edward's voice came again softer this time. "No, there's no one else in the house. Are you almost done?"

"Yes, sir, I'm almost finished."

"Hey, what are you doing? Get away from there."

Jordan tensed and tightened his grip on his gun. She must have seen something, but why wouldn't she just use the code word and get out.

"Sir, I was just going to check the cabinets. There's no need to pull a gun out."

Oh crud. The guy had a gun. That was his cue. Waiting any longer might get Cassidy shot. He took a deep breath before jumping through the cracked door and leveling his firearm on the man. "Fire Beach Police Department. Drop your weapon. You're under arrest."

As he'd hoped, his entrance drew Edward's attention away from Cassidy, but now he swung the gun Jordan's direction.

"Drop your weapon," Jordan repeated. He did not want to fire on this man. Not in an apartment building where bullets could go through walls and not with Cassidy so close.

Edward lowered his arm as if he were going to comply, but then a cold gleam appeared in his eyes and his arm shot back up. Jordan watched the scene as if in slow motion knowing he could either fire and risk getting shot or get out of the way but not both.

He was a good shot, but firing could injure Cassidy or the kid as he still wasn't sure what she had seen. Plus, Edward's bullet might hit him as well, but getting out of the way might give Edward time to turn the gun on Cassidy.

Before Jordan could decide, he saw Cassidy's leg shoot out and connect with the flesh right behind Edward's knee. As the man stumbled, his arm jerked up and the piercing sound of a gunshot filled the air, but it gave Jordan the time he needed. Sprinting forward, he tackled Edward to the ground and kicked his gun away. Edward protested and attempted to throw Jordan off his back, but the attack had caught him off guard and Jordan was able to wrestle Edward's arms behind him.

"Edward Long, you're under arrest," he said as he secured the handcuffs.

"What for?" Edward asked belligerently. "She's the trespasser. She was snooping in my apartment."

Cassidy walked over by the cabinets and pulled at the paneling on the wall revealing three small children trapped inside. "For kidnapping would be my guess."

"I'm going to say we can probably tack on human trafficking," Jordan added as he gazed at the children who huddled together and stared at Cassidy with fearful eyes. He hated the terror that covered the faces of these children, but he was relieved that all of them had been found. It didn't often work out that way, but Long must have been waiting for more money or had issues getting them offloaded. Whatever the reason, he sent a silent thank you to God for watching over the two boys and girl who couldn't be older than eight before spouting the rest of the Miranda rights at Edward Long.

"I'll bet we'll even be able to add on assault and arson, won't we?"

Edward turned his head and snarled up at them. "That woman had it coming. Always knocking at my apartment. She should have just left the mail in my box or under my doorstep."

"You might want to take that right to remain silent,"

Jordan said as he reached into his pocket and pulled out his phone dialing the numbers to reach dispatch. "This is Detective Jordan Graves with the Special Investigation Unit. I need two ambulances and a backup to transport a prisoner to 452 Wheeler Avenue. Call Stone."

Cassidy crouched down and addressed the kids in a soft voice. "Don't worry guys. You're safe now. I'm a firefighter. See my uniform? Can you come out?"

One at a time, the kids crawled out of the small space and clutched onto Cassidy. Rage roared inside Jordan and the urge to punch the man beneath him fought to escape. How dare this man take these children from their parents? How dare he try to sell them for money? How dare he keep them shut up in the walls like animals?

But punching the man wouldn't solve the problem and it would probably frighten the children even more than they were. So, he wouldn't. Instead, he turned his attention to Cassidy. "You did good." She was impressive, and as much as he still feared losing his heart again, his objections were beginning to seem less important.

She shook her head and squeezed the children tighter. "No, we did good."

CHAPTER 10

Jordan watched the paramedics load the children into the ambulance before turning to Cassidy. "How did you know they were in there?"

Cassidy shook her head, but she didn't look at him. Her focus remained on the children. "I didn't for sure. I saw that the paneling was separated from the wall and it just reminded me of the hole I saw at the fire. When he got jumpy as I approached it, I knew he had to be hiding something."

Before Jordan could tell her how lucky she was Edward hadn't fired on her, Stone approached. "Good job, Jordan. We'll get the kids reunited with their parents tonight and I'll see if we can get our friend here to talk.

He can't be working alone." Stone turned to face Cassidy. "I hear we owe this break to you."

"Oh, I don't know if you can attribute the whole break to me." She smiled up at Jordan. "Jordan was the one who remembered the name and came in with guns blazing."

Stone lifted an eyebrow as he glanced from Cassidy to Jordan and back again. "Yes, well, he's lucky things turned out the way they did. Next time he should remember to call for backup though."

Jordan took the criticism with a nod. He knew there would probably be another stern reprimand in his future, but he was grateful Stone didn't do it in front of Cassidy.

Stone turned his attention back to Cassidy. "Thank you for the help you supplied in this case. I'll make sure your captain knows about it. Word on the street is that he wasn't too happy when you took time off to do your show, but maybe this will allow him to ease up on you. Jordan, why don't you take tomorrow off? I think you deserve a rest day."

"Thank you, sir." Jordan wasn't sure he'd get any rest though. Graham had texted him earlier asking him to meet to go over the interior layout of the restaurant, and he still needed to investigate Cassidy's stalker.

Beside him, Cassidy spoke up. "Um, before you go, sir. I have a doll that belonged to the girl at the firehouse.

I'd like to get it back to her. Do you know how long they'll be at the hospital?"

"I'm not positive, but if you get it there tonight, I'm sure it will get to the owner." With that, Stone walked back to the squad car that held Edward Long.

"Not the talkative type, is he?" Cassidy asked.

Jordan chuckled. "Not really, but he is good at his job." He turned to face Cassidy and his breath caught as he gazed into her eyes. He'd felt something in the apartment when he'd seen the gun pointed at her. This fear of her getting hurt. And he'd reacted without thinking, which was dangerous. He should break contact now and run, but his body wouldn't move.

She returned his stare, and her lips parted as if begging for him to kiss them. His body screamed at him to take her in his arms and do just that, but he muffled the shouts and told himself they would never work out though he was no longer sure exactly why. "It's getting late. I should probably take you back to the hospital."

The sparkle in her eyes dimmed, and her mouth formed a thin line. Jordan knew he had hurt her. He hadn't meant to, but a little hurt now was much better than a lot of hurt later. "Look, Cassidy, I'm not good at this stuff…" His voice was stilled by the placement of her lips against his.

For a moment, he was too surprised to react, but then his brain kicked into gear and his hands moved from her arms to her neck, his fingers tangling in her hair. Her hands pulled at the back of his neck as if trying to draw his face closer. Then suddenly, she pulled back.

"You want to tell me you felt nothing?" she asked when the kiss ended. Her breathing was irregular and he could hear the pounding of her heart. Or his? He was no longer sure of anything it seemed.

He opened his mouth, but he couldn't tell her that he'd felt nothing. Nothing was definitely *not* what he'd felt. A spark of heat flowing from his head to his toes and an overwhelming sense of peace that hadn't graced him in a year – those he had felt, but was it enough? Was it enough to throw caution to the wind and give love another chance?

"Never mind," Cassidy said before he could find words. "I shouldn't have done that. I know relationships that begin from dangerous situations rarely last, but I just couldn't help myself."

"I just…" He should tell her, explain his hesitation, but the words wouldn't come. He wasn't even sure what his hesitation was any more. Was he really worried she would be like Jasmine? "I can't right now."

"It's fine." She stepped away from him, crossed her arms over her chest as if building a wall between them. "Can you just take me back to the firehouse so I can get the doll? Then you can drop me at the hospital."

"Cassidy, I…" but he had nothing. He wasn't ready

to open up the past yet and that meant closing this door. For now. With a sigh, he led the way back to his car.

"Is THAT JORDAN?" Ivy whispered with wide eyes as Cassidy grabbed the doll off her bunk.

"Yes, now stop staring. He's going to think something's wrong with you." Cassidy's voice came in a hushed hiss. She was still berating herself for kissing Jordan. What had she been thinking? Well, she hadn't. That was the problem. She'd been swept up in the moment and following her heart and just like with Tyler and David, she had put it out there only to get it rejected. Again.

"Something is wrong with me." Ivy began to fan herself with her hand. "My heart is beating like crazy, and I feel like someone turned up the heat. Ooh, girl, he is fine on the eyes."

"Stop it," Cassidy said swatting her friend's hand. She'd made a big enough fool of herself tonight; she didn't need Ivy making it worse.

Ivy snapped out of her teasing banter but wasn't done with the topic yet. "He's so handsome. No wonder you didn't care about the doctor or the jump start guy."

Scott. With all the excitement of finding Edward Long, Cassidy still hadn't given Jordan the information on Scott or Dustin for that matter. Would he still look into her stalker? Or would he pass her off to someone else to avoid the tension that now lived between them. "Yes, he's handsome. He's also waiting for me, so we'll discuss this more later."

"Have fun." Ivy flashed her a wink and a mischievous smile.

Cassidy shook her head as she returned to Jordan who stood in the doorway of the bunk room looking uncomfortable. "Sorry about her," she said in explanation, "Ivy means well, but sometimes she gets a little…"

"Zealous?" he finished for her.

"Yeah, that would be a good word, but I got what I came for, so let's get back to the hospital before they release whoever this belongs to."

As they drove to the hospital, Cassidy debated whether to bring up Scott again or not. She didn't want to worsen the mood, but her stalker was still out there. As she opened her mouth to broach the topic, the hospital came into view on their left. It could wait.

A different woman was working the station this time, but Jordan's badge granted them admission. The children's rooms were all in a row, and Cassidy and Jordan popped their head into the first one. A small girl was asleep in the bed, but her parents sat vigil by her and they glanced up.

"Sorry, we didn't mean to disturb you," Jordan said before they could say anything. "I'm Detective Graves and this is Firefighter Marcel who found your daughter. We're looking for a little girl who might have lost a doll."

Cassidy held the doll up and the woman brought her hand to her mouth. "That's Baby. Sophie's been crying for her since we got here. Where did you find her?"

"I found Baby at the scene of a fire," Cassidy said, her voice choked with emotion. "I'm sorry she's in such bad shape, but she's actually the reason we found the children."

A soft sob escaped the woman, and her husband wrapped an arm around her shoulders. "I'm sorry," he said wiping a tear from his eye, "we're so grateful. It's just a lot to take in."

"It is," Jordan said stepping forward, "but there are places that can help." He pulled out his wallet and handed over a business card. "This place has great counseling for situations like this. Please don't hesitate to use them."

The man nodded, and Cassidy stepped forward and handed the doll to the woman. "I don't know if she'll still want it since I'm sure it doesn't look the same, but you can tell her how brave Baby was."

"Thank you. Thank you for finding our daughter."

"You're welcome." Though Cassidy sometimes saw

survivors after a fire, this case felt different. Heavier. More rewarding.

"Is it always like that?" Cassidy asked as they stepped back into the hallway.

"When the outcome is good? Yes."

Cassidy didn't ask what it was like when the outcome wasn't as good. She'd seen that first hand as well. They walked in silence back to the parking lot and to her car. "You didn't have to walk me out," she said.

"Actually," he sighed and jammed his hands in his coat pockets, "I did. Cassidy, I need to explain."

Her heart began to pound in her chest as she leaned against her car. Jordan stepped closer closing the distance, but Cassidy didn't move. Even when his fingers touched her cheek and tucked a strand of hair behind her ear, she didn't break her gaze from his mesmerizing stare.

"You caught me off guard tonight, Cassidy, and that is hard to do."

"I'm sorry..." She didn't get to finish the apology as his finger touched her lips silencing her and sending waves of emotion through her body.

"I've spent a lot of time building up emotional walls. My last relationship ended in the worst way possible. She thought she wanted to marry a cop, but on our wedding day, she realized she didn't and never showed."

Cassidy's eyes widened, but she said nothing sensing

that he needed to continue and get whatever he wanted to say off his chest.

"I haven't dated since." His fingers slid down her neck to the top of her shoulder. "I thought I was done with love, but you awakened something in me with that kiss. I just need some time to process. Can you give me that?"

Cassidy nodded. She didn't want to give him time. She wanted to pull him to her and taste his lips again, but if time was what he needed, she would give it. "Jordan, before you go. I know Stone gave you tomorrow off, but if I send you Scott's information, can you look into him when you get back to work?"

"Of course I will. I want any information you have on the guy in your apartment complex too, and Cassidy?" She stared up at him mesmerized by the look in his eyes. "If anything else happens – letters, phone calls, a feeling - I want you to call me. No matter what time it is. Don't let this thing between us stop you from calling. Promise?"

"I promise."

He raked a thumb across her cheek. "Good, now go home and get some sleep. I'll call you tomorrow." His lips touched against hers, softly, not like their first kiss, but the simple touch still sent a shiver down her spine. There was no doubt in her mind. She was falling for Jordan Graves.

He waited until she was in her car with the motor running before he walked back to his own car. With a smile on her face, Cassidy pulled out of the parking lot and began the drive back to her house. It was still early, not even six. Maybe she would take a long bubble bath before cooking dinner and then curl up with a good book.

But her smile faltered as a bang sounded, and her car began to pull to the right. Had she blown a tire? How? She'd seen nothing in the road. With all her might, she yanked the steering wheel to the left but it was no use. The car was stronger than she was and continued to pull to the right. She fumbled for her phone hoping to dial 911, but as she got it out of her pocket, the car hit the curb, and the phone flew from her hand and landed on the floorboard. Cassidy had no time to grab it though because at that moment, something rammed her from behind and her head slammed on the steering wheel.

CHAPTER 11

"Why do you look so cranky?" Graham asked as Jordan shrugged out of his coat and laid it across the bar.

"What do you mean? This is how I always look." He took his gun out of the holster and laid it on the jacket.

Graham shook his head as he pulled out a blueprint design and spread it on the table. "No, you look meaner today. More agitated."

Jordan sighed and paced away from the table. He hadn't slept much the night before as he'd lain awake thinking about what to do with Cassidy. His mind would list all the reasons they would never work out, but then his heart would speed up just thinking about her. "It's this woman, Cassidy. She's a firefighter, and she's amazing. Even helped me solve the big kidnapping case I was working on."

"So, what's the problem? She sounds perfect for you."

Jordan ran a hand through his hair and let out an exasperated breath. "The problem is that she reminds me of Jasmine, you know, the other woman you thought was perfect for me."

Graham's head shot up, a hurt expression on his face. "Hey, you can't blame that on me. She was perfect for you. If you hadn't been a cop."

Jordan threw his hands up and rolled his eyes. "But I am a cop! And what happens if Cassidy turns out to be the same?" He didn't think he could put his heart out there again.

Graham folded his arms and leaned back. "Okay, so that's the worst that could happen. What's the best that could happen?"

"What?"

"I mean if she doesn't turn out to be like Jasmine, what could life be like?"

Jordan shook his head and raked a hand across his cheek. "I don't know. She's a firefighter and I'm a cop. Our schedules would probably never work. And her job is nearly as dangerous as mine. That's no way to raise a family."

"But?"

Jordan frowned at Graham. Why was he pushing this? "But when she kissed me, I felt alive. For the first time since Jasmine."

Graham shrugged and leaned back over the blueprint. "So, I guess the question you need to ask yourself is if it's worth it. Are the fears and the hardships worth feeling alive again?"

Jordan narrowed his eyes at his brother. They didn't talk about their dating lives much, but the last he knew his brother was single, so when did he get so insightful? "When did you get your counseling degree?"

Graham glanced up. "I didn't. I'm actually sharing something Dad said to me before he passed."

Jordan tensed at the words. He wasn't sure he wanted any advice from his father.

"Hear me out," Graham continued holding up a hand. "You know he tried really hard to be sober the last few years. He wasn't perfect, but he was trying. One day, he told me he was having a hard time. Only he wasn't talking about women. He was talking about his next drink. He could stay sober and live with the pain of what he'd done, who'd he'd hurt, or he could let the drink take that pain away."

Before he could stop the words, Jordan opened his mouth. "What did he choose?"

"He chose to feel the pain, to own up to his mistakes. I know you don't want to be like him, but he wasn't all bad, Jordan. He let alcohol take ahold of his life and that ruined him. Don't let the fear of heartbreak do the same to you."

Jordan wanted to argue, but what Graham was saying made sense. Fear wasn't the same as alcohol, but he could see how if he let it control his life, his opportunities, that it could have the same hold on him. He walked to the table and scanned the blueprint. "You might be right."

Graham leaned forward as well. "I know I'm right. Anyway, all I'm saying is that you can't live your life in fear. What if this firefighter is the one you're supposed to be with and you never give her a chance? Now, can we pick an interior design?" Graham pointed to the blueprints spread out on the table. "I'd like to get started on this as soon as possible."

Jordan chuckled at his brother's abrupt switch in topic. Now that he'd had his say, he was all ready to get down to business. "Yeah, just give me one second to call her and see if she can meet up later."

Having made the decision to give love a shot, he suddenly couldn't wait to see Cassidy again. He pulled out his cell phone and dialed her number. At nearly nine thirty in the morning, he expected to hear her voice pick up, but the phone simply rang. And rang. Until finally her voice mail clicked on. He listened all the way through it and then left his message. "Cassidy, it's Jordan.

I was hoping maybe we could get together today. Please call me when you get this message." He hung up, briefly wondering where she might be but sure she would call him back when she received the message.

"Okay," he said walking back toward Graham. "Show me what you've got."

CASSIDY MOANED as she struggled to open her eyes. Her head hurt though she wasn't exactly sure why. In fact, her whole body felt stiff and sore. She touched her forehead wincing as her fingers pressed on a raised bump. Where had that come from?

Then it came back to her. She was on her way home from the hospital when her tire had blown and then something had hit her car. She'd hit the steering wheel which explained the bump on her head, but why wasn't she still in her car?

Was she in the hospital then? Her eyes opened the rest of the way and she took in the room – what little of it she could see in the dim light. She was in a bed, but this was not a hospital room. The dark walls were nothing like the sterile white of a hospital, and the one window in the room was boarded over allowing only a sliver of light into the room.

She pushed herself to a sitting position gritting her

teeth against the pounding pain in her head. There was nothing in the room beside the bed and a pail against the wall. Was that where she was supposed to relieve herself? The door was solid metal except for a rectangular panel that appeared to open and close. This wasn't a room. It was a cage. Her stalker must have found her.

When the throbbing in her head lessened, Cassidy stood and walked to the window. The boards were nailed on the outside, so she couldn't even try to pry them off from in here. She supposed she could try to break the glass and push on them, but she didn't know what the noise might bring. Also, there was no way to bandage herself if she cut herself on broken glass from the window, and she had no desire to bleed out in this depressing room.

Fear tightened in her chest. How was she going to get out of here? She wasn't expected at work today so no one would even know she was missing until tomorrow unless they found her car. And even if they did, how would they know where to begin looking for her? She didn't even know where she was.

A scraping sound drew her attention back to the metal door. "Who's there?" she called out. "Where am I?"

There was no verbal answer, just a gloved hand appearing with a bowl. Cassidy couldn't even tell if the hand belonged to a man or a woman though she suspected a man. Not wanting to give her captor the satisfaction of knowing she was hungry even though she was starving, she simply waited.

"Grab the bowl." The voice was deep and gravelly, but also machine like. He was altering his voice.

"No. Let me out of here."

"You will eat," the voice commanded.

Cassidy crossed her arms enjoying the power it gave her even though her captor couldn't see them. Her stomach ached and rumbled displeased at having missed dinner the night before, but she wasn't going to let him know that. "You can't make me."

"Suit yourself." The hand let go of the bowl and it dropped to the floor. The bowl didn't break, but the contents, which looked like runny oatmeal, spilled out on the floor. Then the rectangular door closed.

Cassidy walked back to the bed and curled her knees to her chest. She would have to eat sooner or later or she wouldn't have the strength to attempt an escape if the opportunity arose. Tears filled her eyes and a vice closed on her throat. How was she going to get out of here?

She turned her face to the ceiling and did the only thing she could do. She prayed.

CHAPTER 12

*J*ordan glanced at his watch. Four hours had passed since he called Cassidy and there had been no reply. Was she angry at him for the day before? Had she been called into work? Work. He could call her work and see if she was there. Jordan typed the firehouse into his search engine and dialed the number that popped up.

"Fire Beach Firehouse, how may I direct your call?" the woman on the other end asked in a pleasant voice.

"Is Cassidy Marcel on today?"

"I'm sorry, sir, I can't give that information out." The pleasantness had dropped from her voice and she was all business now.

Of course, he should have known they wouldn't give out personal information. "I apologize; this is Detective

Jordan Graves with the FBPD. I'm investigating her stalker case and need to speak with her, but she isn't answering her phone. If she's there, can you connect me?"

"I'm sorry, Detective, she isn't on shift today, and I haven't seen her."

Jordan hung up the phone without saying goodbye and chewed on his bottom lip. Maybe it meant nothing. Maybe she'd decided to unplug and lay low, but he didn't think so. His gut was churning again, and it was telling him something had happened to her.

"What's wrong?" Graham asked as Jordan paced the room.

"I'm not sure. Cassidy hasn't returned my call, and I'm worried about her."

"Dude, maybe she's just busy." Graham rolled up the blueprint they had chosen and secured it with a rubber band. "I think you're overreacting."

It was possible, but Jordan didn't think so. His gut was rarely wrong, and right now it was twisting and turning into knots. "Maybe, but I met Cassidy because she had a stalker. What if he found her? What if something happened to her?"

A look of sympathy crossed Graham's features. "We're done here. Why don't you go see if she's home and lying low?"

"Thanks, man." Jordan strapped his gun back in

place and shoved his arms into his jacket. It was ten minutes to her apartment and each minute seemed like eternity. He was tempted to throw on his lights and sirens to get people to move out of the way, but this wasn't an emergency. Yet.

A broken lamppost appeared on his right and snagged his attention. He didn't remember seeing it before and while it might mean nothing, the hair on the back of his neck now stood at attention. He pulled the car over and stepped out.

The dent in the lamppost held a streak of red – the same color as Cassidy's car. His eyes dropped to the ground, and he spied broken plastic and streaks on the curb as if tires had rubbed against them. There had obviously been an accident here but where was the car?

Jordan pulled out his phone and dialed Stone.

Stone's gruff voice filled his ear. "Jordan? I thought I told you to take the day off."

Jordan shook his head. He didn't have time for explanations. "You did, but, sir, I think something's happened to Cassidy Marcel. Can you see if DOT transported a wrecked vehicle from 72nd and Trosper last night or this morning?"

"Hold on. I'll check." This was why he liked working for Stone. The man knew when to ask questions and when to trust his officers. "Yeah, they towed it this morning to lot A. Said no one was inside."

"Thank you, sir. I'll be in touch soon."

Jordan jumped back in his car and turned it around. Lot A wasn't too far away. He just hoped he would find some answers there. "Hold on, Cassidy, I'm coming."

CASSIDY STARED at the walls around her and wondered how much time had passed. Her watch was missing, probably taken, and she didn't have her phone. She had nothing but silence and four walls.

For a while, she had prayed, but soon her words ran out. Not that she thought God wasn't still listening – she was sure He was – but she could only ask Him to save her so many times. Then she'd tried to sleep, but hunger had started gnawing its way up her stomach. The smell of the runny oatmeal on the floor hadn't helped.

The sound of scraping metal came again and Cassidy hurried to the door hoping to catch a glimpse of the room outside. She didn't know what she'd do with the information as she had no way to get out of the room she was in or tell anyone where she was, but the tiny room was closing in on her, and she needed to know there was more out there to regain her sanity.

"Please, let me out of here," she said as she squatted down to try and see out of the rectangle. A pair of legs clad in denim appeared before another plate of food filled the window. This time a sandwich and a bag of chips.

"I can't let you out until I've convinced you we belong together." The voice was still altered but Cassidy was sure she'd heard it before.

"You've convinced me," she tried. "We belong together. Now, please let me out."

"Nice try, but I haven't yet. Take the food."

Well, it had been worth a shot. "No, I'm not taking anything from you. You'll have to watch me die in here and then we'll never be together."

"You will eat." Once again, the plate dropped and the window slid shut. The sandwich landed in the oatmeal – guess she wasn't eating that – but the bag of chips managed to avoid the brown mess. Cassidy had no intention of breaking them open right now, but they were bagged. It would be harder to poison something bagged, so she plucked them up and took them to the bed. Chips weren't enough to sustain energy for long, but she was not going to die in here.

CHAPTER 13

*J*ordan opened the door of Cassidy's car and tried not to dwell on the worst-case scenario as he spied the dried blood on the steering wheel. She'd probably hit her head or her face, both of which tended to bleed more than other areas. It was clear from the car that something had hit her from behind, probably pushing her into the lamppost.

There was no other blood on the seat or anywhere else which gave Jordan some hope. He moved farther into the car searching for anything that might give him a clue as to what had happened to her. Nothing in the seats caught his attention other than the fact that her bag still sat in the passenger seat.

He opened it feeling as if he shouldn't be snooping in it but knowing it was necessary. Her wallet was still there and when he popped the snap, he saw her credit cards and cash still inside. So, this wasn't a robbery. He hadn't thought it was but finding this confirmed it.

A glance in the backseat revealed nothing new there either, but Jordan hoped Cassidy would have left him some clue if she could have. He backed out of the car and bent down to check the floorboard. There his eyes landed on her phone. He plucked it off the mat hoping he would be able to access it. She had never sent him the text with the information on the possible stalkers and now it might hold the only clues.

He pressed his finger to the power circle, but the keypad screen came up. Darn it. He didn't know her well enough to have any idea what her password might be, but he knew someone who might.

After examining the car one more time to make sure he hadn't missed anything, Jordan shut her door and hurried back to his own car. Ten minutes later, he pulled into the firehouse parking lot. He just hoped Ivy would be working.

The same woman he had met a few days before was at the desk. "Can I help you?"

"I need to speak to the paramedic. Ivy something or other. I'm sorry I don't know her last name, but it's important I speak with her."

His eyes must have shown the frazzled sense of

urgency he felt in his bones because the woman picked up the phone and paged Ivy Hopkins.

She appeared a moment later, her blonde hair pulled back in a loose ponytail and a quizzical expression on her face. "Jordan? What can I do for you?"

He held out Cassidy's phone and watched as Ivy's eyes widened. "Do you know how to unlock it?"

"Why do you have this?" Fear threaded her voice and her eyes darted around as if she thought he might harm her.

"Cassidy's missing. I found this in her car. She never sent me the information about the possible stalker, but she said she had the man's name and number in her phone. So, can you open it?"

"Um, I think so. She told me what it was once." Ivy grabbed the phone and closed her eyes. Her face scrunched in thought. Jordan wanted to shake her and tell her to hurry up, but he knew that would accomplish nothing, so he waited. Ivy's eyes popped open and she tapped a few numbers in the phone. "No, that's not it." She tapped the screen again and a triumphant smile lit up her face. "Got it."

Jordan snatched the phone from her and clicked on the message icon. There was no draft to him, so she hadn't even started forming the message yet. He supposed that made sense since she had been taken before she got home, but it didn't keep him from kicking himself for not getting the information from her before he let her go.

"What was the guy's name?" As he scrolled through her contacts, he realized she had never told him the guy's name. Why hadn't he asked better questions?

"The guy who stopped by here with the flowers?" Ivy asked.

Jordan's eyes shot to her. "Yes, did she tell you his name?"

"Yeah, his name was Scott. I was there when she exchanged numbers with him."

Scott. He flicked the scrolling arrow to get to the eses. Yes, there it was. He took out his own phone to take a picture of the number. "Could you describe him?"

"Of course. He was handsome, but kind of nerdy with the glasses and all."

"Great, I need you to come to the station with me and describe him to a sketch artist. What about the other guy?"

Ivy's forehead furrowed as she shook her head. "What other guy?"

"The one at her apartment. She said there was a guy who seemed odd at her apartment complex. One who walked his dog and stared at her."

"Dustin? I'm pretty sure he's harmless. He's always walking his dog outside. I spoke to him once or twice when I was checking on her apartment for her."

Suddenly her eyes widened. "Oh my gosh, could he be the stalker?"

"I don't know yet, but I'm going to investigate them both."

Ivy's face paled and her hand covered her mouth. Jordan knew that look. "What?" he asked.

"I just… I thought they were friends, so I talked about her when he asked. Like he wanted to know why I was there and I told him I was watching her apartment while she was on the show. Did I do this? Did I get her kidnapped?" Her eyes took on a vacant stare.

Jordan had no time to console the woman, but he knew she was beating herself up. "We don't know who the stalker is yet, so stop blaming yourself and let's find this guy. Can you come to the station with me now?"

"What?" Ivy blinked a few times bringing her eyes back into focus. "Yes, just let me tell Captain Fitzgerald what's going on. I'll be right back."

As she dashed off, Jordan checked his watch. Cassidy had been missing for nearly twenty-four hours and he didn't want it to be any longer. He had to find her.

CASSIDY'S STOMACH rumbled again as she turned on the hard bed. The light in the room was fading which meant evening was approaching. Her mouth was dry from not drinking all day and she could already feel the lack of food taking a toll on her. How much longer would she be here? Had anyone found her car yet? Did they know she was missing? Would Jordan hunt for her? He'd admitted there was an attraction but then he'd said he needed time. What if that meant days? No, she couldn't think like that. She needed to stay focused and positive.

The rectangle slid open again, but this time Cassidy didn't scramble over to try and peer out. She knew the view was limited and she didn't want to give this guy the satisfaction of seeing her. "Dinner."

"I'm not hungry," Cassidy said though the ache in her stomach protested.

"You will eat."

She had tried begging and lying. Neither had worked, but Cassidy wondered if bribery might. "I'll eat if you'll tell me who you are."

"You shouldn't have to ask," the voice growled.

Ouch! She'd touched a nerve, but she wasn't going to stop now. She wasn't sure what she would gain by knowing the identity of her captor, but she needed to know. "But I do. You're disguising your voice and you haven't shown me your face, so how would I know who you are?"

"I sent you the letters."

"Yes, but you didn't put your name on them or a return address, so how could I know it was you?"

"I left you other gifts." The agitation in his voice increased with every answer, but Cassidy felt fairly safe locked in this room.

"At the fire station?" There'd been a few gifts in the bag, mostly chocolates which she had thrown out even though she loved chocolate.

"No, on your doorstep."

Cassidy sucked in her breath. So, he knew where she lived. That had to make it Dustin unless Scott had followed her home without her knowing it. "What gifts? I never received any on my doorstep." She thought back over the last few months, but she couldn't remember anything being outside her door.

"You're lying. You did get them and after everything I've done for you, I can't believe you're saying you don't remember or that you kissed that guy. I know you didn't mean it, but I'm the only guy you're supposed to be kissing." He dropped the plate spilling the soup and bread onto the floor before slamming the rectangle shut again.

So, he'd seen her yesterday with Jordan. That made sense. Seeing her kiss another man would probably push him over the edge enough to abduct her, but that still didn't tell her who *he* was. Her gut was telling her it was Dustin, but what had he meant by gifts? She hadn't been lying about that; she'd never received any gifts at her apartment. At least not that she knew of. She lay back on the bed and tried to go over every interaction she had ever had with Dustin.

Generally, she saw him on her way to or from work when he'd be walking his dog outside. There was the one time he'd offered to wash her windows, but she'd declined. She hadn't wanted him that close to her windows, and the landlord had a company that came out once every few months to clean up the outside of the apartments.

The gifts still bothered her. What if he had put the gifts on the wrong doorstep? But Dustin knew which apartment was hers; she was sure of it. Did that mean it was Scott then? Maybe he'd followed her to the parking lot but hadn't seen which building she entered? That didn't make much sense though because if he was stalking her, why wouldn't he watch her walk all the way inside?

He just hadn't given her enough clues to be sure, but Cassidy would keep trying.

CHAPTER 14

"Jordan? What are you doing-" Al's voice faded as she spied Ivy behind him. "Who's that?"

"This is Ivy Hopkins. She's a friend of Cassidy's and a paramedic who works out of the firehouse. Cassidy's been taken, and she's here to help identify the possible suspects." Jordan sat down at his desk and turned the computer on.

"Whoa! What?"

Jordan could understand Al's confusion, but he didn't have time to explain it. He typed the cell number into the database and waited for the information to pop up. Scott Cline 5554 Wagoneer Avenue.

"Is that him?" Ivy asked peering over his shoulder.

"Is that who?" Al asked coming around the desk to see the computer.

"The guy who came to the firehouse," Ivy said. "Evidently, Cassidy gave him a jumpstart and then he showed up later with flowers and a dinner invite, so we think he might be her stalker."

"A possible suspect," Jordan corrected, "and I don't know yet. Let me put this in the DMV site and see if there's a picture." Jordan pulled up the website and plugged in the information. A moment later, a picture filled the screen. He turned the monitor toward Ivy. "Is it?"

Ivy nodded. "Yeah, that's definitely him. Is he the stalker?"

"I can start a background check, but it's going to take some time to get results back. In the meantime, I'll visit Scott's home and see if he'll talk to me. Then I want to stop by Cassidy's apartment and see what else I can find out about Dustin. You don't know his last name, do you?"

Ivy's head shook slowly, sadly. "I don't. I never asked much about him."

"Can you at least tell me what he looked like?"

Ivy shrugged. "Bland. He has sandy brown hair, about your height, thin. Nothing that would stand out. Maybe I should go with you to help identify him."

"No, you're staying here. The landlord should be

able to help." He glanced at his watch. It was after five. "Except the office is probably closed. Do you have the landlord's number?"

"No, but I think it was on the door for emergencies. I know it was on Cassidy's fridge." She reached into her purse and pulled out her keys. "I have her apartment key if you need it."

Jordan stared at the key. He didn't want to go in Cassidy's apartment. Not without her permission and not with the emotions running rampant through his body right now. "I'll take my chances on the number first. If it's not on the door, I can find it out another way. Al, call me when the background on Scott Cline comes in."

"I'm going with you."

"No, I need you here to give me the information. Cassidy's already been missing nearly a whole day. We have to move fast and that means I need someone I can trust getting me the information I need."

Al held his gaze for a minute as if debating whether to argue with him or not. "Fine," she said and sat down in his vacated seat.

"Thanks Al. I'll get you a complete name as soon as I talk to the landlord." He headed for the exit and pushed open the door.

A few minutes later, he turned left on Wagoneer and pulled to a stop in front of 5554. An old Mustang was parked in the driveway, and Jordan hoped that meant Scott Cline was home.

The door swung open to reveal the man from the photos. "Scott Cline?"

"Yeah?" The man's voice was hesitant as his eyes scanned Jordan's face.

"I'm Detective Graves, and I need to ask you a few questions about Cassidy Marcel." Jordan pulled his jacket aside to display his badge.

The man's eyes flicked down to the badge and then back up to Jordan. "Who?"

"Cassidy, the firefighter you brought flowers to."

Scott blinked, nodded, and pushed the glasses up the bridge of his nose. "Oh, okay. I don't really know her. She helped me jump my car and I brought her flowers and asked her to dinner. I tried calling the number she gave me, but it was the wrong one. I just figured she wasn't interested."

"Unfortunately, she's gone missing, so I'm hoping you can tell me where you were yesterday."

Scott's eyes widened and he took a step back. "I didn't have anything to do with that. I was at work all day yesterday. You can check with my office. I had another big meeting, so I was there at seven a.m. and didn't leave until after nine p.m."

Jordan ran through the timeline in his head. He had left Cassidy before six p.m. and she had never texted him which made him think the accident had occurred shortly after she left him. "Can I get your work information to verify?"

Scott rattled off the information and Jordan plugged it into his phone. He would have Al verify it, but his gut told him Scott was not the man.

"Listen, I hope you find her, but if you do, tell her I'm no longer interested. I don't need this kind of drama in my life." He stepped back and closed the door.

Jordan fought the urge to knock on the door again and give the guy a piece of his mind, but that would do nothing to help Cassidy. This guy didn't seem to be the captor and the timeline didn't fit. He was a jerk but nothing more. Which meant that the best suspect right now was Dustin.

While it was possible he was dealing with a total unknown person, the statistics behind stalking suggested it was someone who knew Cassidy, and Dustin asking about her was a classic sign of stalking which made him wonder if this escalation was his fault.

Could Dustin have been at Edward Long's apartment or the hospital and seen them kiss? If he had, it might explain the abduction. Dustin would have been angry that Cassidy was seeing someone else and that might have led to the aggressive behavior. If that was the case, Jordan was responsible for this event. He had put an innocent woman in danger, and he had to make it right.

"DUSTIN?" Cassidy banged on the door and hollered at the top of her lungs. "Dustin, let me out of here so we can talk." She still wasn't positive Dustin was her stalker, but after reviewing what she knew, the scale tipped in his favor. "Dustin?" She pounded again and the rectangle slid open. "Dustin, let's talk about this."

"So, you finally realized it was me." His voice modulator was gone, and Cassidy recognized the voice immediately. The sound had never given her warm fuzzies but it sent shivers down her spine now.

"I did, but I still have questions for you. I was hoping you could answer them. I know you don't owe me any explanation since you've done so much for me already, but it would help me." Cassidy hoped she was hitting the right buttons. She'd never had to deal with a stalker before, but the cop shows she watched stated stalkers usually made up stories in their heads of what they thought happened.

"What do you want to know?"

"Why did you send the letters to the firehouse? Why not leave them on my doorstep?"

"Because you never said anything about all the other

letters I left on your doorstep. When I heard you'd gone on the show, I thought maybe if I sent the letters to your work, you would know how serious I was."

Other letters? Cassidy had no knowledge of other letters. "I never got them, Dustin – the ones you left on my doorstep. I'm sorry; I would have acknowledged them if I had." She probably would have run to the police and filed a restraining order, but she would have acknowledged them.

"I don't believe you," he roared and pounded on the door with such force that Cassidy took a step back. "I told you in those letters how much I loved you and how we belonged together and you went on that stupid dating show anyway. That's not how you show love."

"You're right, but I promise you that I never received any letters or gifts from you at my apartment. I only got the letters and gifts at the station and since you didn't sign them, I didn't know who to thank. Please, can you let me out so we can discuss this?" Cassidy held her breath as she waited. She didn't know what she would find on the other side, but it had to be better than this tiny room.

"I'll think about it." And then the rectangle closed again and Cassidy was left in the silence once more. Only now, the light was officially gone, and the room was dark. Dark and silent. She didn't know how much longer she could take it.

CHAPTER 15

*J*ordan pulled into the apartment parking lot and parked in front of the darkened office. He hoped the landlord's number was on the door. Twenty-four hours had already passed and Jordan knew the statistics were grim, but he'd beaten the statistics with the children. Maybe he could beat them with Cassidy too. He breathed a slight sigh of relief when he saw the small note on the door that held the landlord's name and phone number.

He punched the numbers into his phone praying the man would be home.

"Hello?"

"Is this Bob Warnke?" Jordan asked.

"It is. What can I help you with?"

"My name is Detective Graves with FBPD and I

need to ask you a few questions. Can you give me your apartment number or meet me at the office?"

"I'll be right there." The phone clicked in Jordan's ear and he ended the call and placed it back in his pocket.

A minute later, a man with fuzzy white hair and a bathrobe shuffled up to him. "I'm Bob. Sorry, I generally retire pretty early. What's this about?"

"It's about one of your tenants," Jordan began. "Do you have a Dustin who rents here? About my height with sandy brown hair? Always walking his dog?"

"That's my nephew, Dustin Gibbs. Has something happened to him?"

Jordan dodged the question and posed his own instead. "Do you know where he is, sir? It's important I find him."

"I'm sure he's in his apartment. Come on, I'll take you there." The man shuffled down the sidewalk to a building two down from Cassidy's. "His apartment is B, but what's this about?"

Jordan knew he needed to tread softly. He didn't want to alarm the man and have him shut down. "I believe Dustin may have information about a missing person I'm searching for."

The man blanched and dropped his eyes as he fumbled with the keys. "Please tell me you don't mean Cassidy Marcel."

A vice squeezed Jordan's heart and he balled his fists to keep from shaking the man. "I do mean Cassidy. She went missing yesterday. What do you know?"

Bob's hands trembled as he flipped through the key ring. "You have to understand Dustin isn't quite right in the head. He's a good kid, but sometimes he gets fixated on things. I saw him talking to Cassidy one day and the next morning I saw him by her apartment. He had left a flower on her doorstep. I didn't want her to freak out, so I took the flower. I thought Dustin would let it go, but he seemed to become obsessed with her. He left at least three more items on her doorstep – notes, flowers, candy."

Jordan's blood boiled in his veins. This man had known and done nothing? "Why didn't you tell Cassidy?" If he had told Cassidy, she could have done something. She could have moved or filed a restraining order. She could have at least known what she was up against.

Bob offered a small shrug. "I didn't think he was dangerous. He never has been before, and I've known him his whole life. In fact, I'm sure it's just a misunderstanding, but I can get him to talk to you." He inserted the key in the door and turned the lock. "Dustin?" he called as he pushed open the door. "Maybe he's sleeping."

Or more likely he wasn't there. Jordan followed the

man into the apartment, his hand close to his gun, but he didn't really expect to use it. Bob continued to call out as he entered the apartment, but when every room had been checked, he sighed. "I guess he's not here."

"Where would he go? Where would he take her?"

Bob scratched his head as the thought. "My sister has an old place a few miles outside of town. No one lives there now, but he could go there I suppose."

"Get me the address. Now."

Jordan placed the call for backup as he sped toward the address. He just hoped they arrived when he did. He wasn't sure he would be able to wait outside knowing Cassidy was so close and probably in danger.

CASSIDY AWOKE with a start when she heard a bang. Had that been a gun shot? Something falling over? She put her ear to the door to try and hear the commotion outside. Had she been found? If it wasn't rescuers, she might jump from the frying pan into the fire if she banged on the door, and someone worse than Dustin found her. Although, right now she couldn't imagine someone worse than Dustin. However, if it was rescuers, she had no idea if they would find her if she didn't pound on the door. She had no reference on where this door was in relation to the rest of the house. There was the one window, so she wasn't completely underground, but it could still be the basement if this was a split-level house.

Deciding the benefits outweighed the drawbacks, Cassidy threw her fists against the metal. "In here. I'm in here. Somebody please help me." There was another crashing sound followed by shouting and then the clear sound of a gunshot. Cassidy's hand froze before banging the door again. She was no longer sure she wanted to be found. The gun could belong to her rescuers, especially if it was the police, but it could also belong to Dustin or someone worse.

Before she could decide, a creaking sound filled the room. The lock turning on the door. Cassidy tried to scan the dark room for anything she could use, but she had nothing. Nothing but a plastic plate and bowl somewhere on the dark floor covered in oatmeal. She backed away from the door and crouched ready to launch herself at whoever came through the door. It wouldn't last long, but maybe she could overpower them with the element of surprise long enough to bolt for the door.

Light flooded the room as the door opened, and with a primal scream, Cassidy threw herself at the body in the doorframe. Only as her eyes adjusted to the light did she realize that the body belonged to Jordan, and by then, she was powerless to stop her force. Her body slammed into his sending him stumbling backward. His arms wrapped around her and he pulled her to his chest as they fell to the floor.

A grunting noise escaped his lips as they landed and then his hands flew to her face. "Are you hurt, Cassidy?"

"Jordan, I'm so sorry. I heard the gunshot and thought Dustin was going to kill me. I figured the element of surprise was my only shot." She ran her hands up his chest where they had landed to his face as if trying to feel out any injured spot.

A small smile played across his lips amid his pained expression. "I'd say you did a good job with that. You might have broken a few of my ribs, but it's worth it to see you safe."

Cassidy knew this was no time for emotions, but she couldn't help placing her lips against his — in apology, in relief, in love.

"I thought you said a relationship that began after a dangerous situation never lasted," he said with a smile as she pulled back.

She returned the smile and resisted the urge to kiss him again. "I decided it was worth it, but I thought you needed more time?"

"My brother convinced me otherwise."

She'd have to thank his brother when she met him, but suddenly she remembered where they were and she looked around. "Where is Dustin?"

"Injured." A woman's voice spoke up. Cassidy glanced around and found a young-looking woman leaning over Dustin and applying pressure to his stomach. "We better get an ambulance here."

Jordan grunted again and pushed Cassidy's hair back. "Cassidy, as much as I love holding you in my arms and want to continue, I need to reach my phone to call for a bus."

Cassidy scrambled off Jordan allowing him to sit up, but her mind wasn't on his phone call. It was on the words he had just said. He loved holding her and wanted to continue.

"How did you find me?" she asked Jordan when he ended his call.

"It's a rather long story," he wheezed as he stood and pulled her to his chest once again. "I promise I'll tell you all about it after we all get checked out. Al, are you okay?"

Al? So, this was his partner?

Al looked up at them an expression of hurt and understanding in her eyes. "I'm fine, but Dustin's vitals are falling. How far out is the ambulance?"

Cassidy thought back to the conversation she had overheard. There had been tension in Jordan's voice when talking about her to Al and from the look in Al's eyes, it was clear she was hurt by their kiss. Did she have feelings for Jordan then? And a better question was did he return them?

"Two minutes."

"Can I help?" Cassidy asked deciding the issue between Al and Jordan could wait for a better time. Dustin might have abducted her and held her hostage, but she didn't want him to die.

"Come help me apply pressure. My arms are starting to shake."

Cassidy took in the room as she crossed to Al. Chairs and tables were overturned and though she hadn't seen what happened, she had a pretty good guess. Jordan and Al had probably surprised Dustin who then kicked over tables and chairs to get away from them, but how had he gotten shot? She couldn't wait to get the full story from Jordan.

CHAPTER 16

"All right, Cassidy, you're all clear," Dr. Brody Cavanaugh said as he finished the exam. "You'll have that bump and a black eye for another few days, but I believe you'll make a full recovery."

"Thank you. Can I go see Jordan now?" Cassidy hadn't wanted to be separated from Jordan when they'd reached the hospital, but the doctors had insisted she get looked at as well even though she'd told them she was fine.

Dr. Cavanaugh smiled and shook his head. "Yes, you can. He's right down the hall in room four."

Cassidy bolted out of the room and down the hall. It seemed like days since she and Jordan had shared that earth-changing kiss, and she didn't want to wait any longer to experience it again.

Jordan sat on the bed trying to get his shirt on, his face twisted in pain.

"Here, let me help you," Cassidy said hurrying to his side and helping him pull the shirt over his head.

"Thank you." He pulled the shirt down over his chiseled abs and then paused as if to catch his breath. "I was hoping you'd come see me." His voice was quieter than normal, but Cassidy wasn't sure if that was the hospital or the broken ribs speaking.

"I couldn't not come visit the man who saved me," Cassidy said as she placed a soft kiss on his cheek. She wanted it to be more but not while his face wrinkled in pain. There would be plenty of time for soul-shattering kisses when his pain lessened.

She sat down beside him on the bed and grabbed his hand. Funny how it still felt rough and strong though he looked so weak in the midst of his pain. "Can I ask you something though?"

"One question first. Did Dustin make it?"

"He did. The bullet missed all his vital organs, and he's getting psychiatric help now."

Jordan nodded. "Good, now what's your question?"

Cassidy took a deep breath. She'd thought about how to ask this but even though she'd rehearsed it, the words still didn't seem right. "Is there something going on between you and Al?"

He narrowed his eyes at her and cocked his head. "Why do you ask?"

"I saw the way she looked at me in the house after we kissed. It's obvious she has feelings for you, but I need to know if you have feelings for her too."

Jordan took her face in his hands. "Al, is my partner, and she means the world to me, but no, I don't have feelings for her like that. Seeing us kiss was probably a shock for her, but she'll get over it. Things will be fine." He leaned forward and placed a soft kiss on her lips.

Cassidy let herself enjoy the taste of his lips, the feel of security, but the story still wasn't complete for her. "Okay, but I have to know. How did you find me?" she asked when he pulled back.

The corners of his mouth pulled into a tight smile, and he took a shallow breath. "Of course you do. Well, when I called you this morning and you didn't return the call, I figured something might be wrong. I drove toward your apartment and saw the light pole you hit, but they had already towed your car. When I found out where it was stored, I searched your car and found your phone. Thankfully, Ivy was able to unlock your screen and get me the information on Scott. I paid him a visit – he's no longer interested just so you know."

"What?" Cassidy placed her hand on her cheek and pretended to be shocked.

"Yeah, he's says you're too much drama now.

Anyway, confident he wasn't your stalker, I spoke to your landlord who admitted he knew Dustin was stalking you. Evidently, he had been leaving gifts on your doorstep but Bob had been removing them before you saw them because he was afraid you would freak out."

Now it all made sense. "So, that's what Dustin meant. He told me he had left me letters and gifts, but I didn't remember receiving any. That's why he switched to sending them to my work."

"Remind me to give that landlord of yours a piece of my mind when these ribs heal," Jordan continued. "Anyway, he gave me the address of the house where Dustin had you and the rest is history."

"Thank you for coming for me." Cassidy traced the veins in his hand relishing the feel of his skin beneath hers.

His lips parted in a soft smile as he lifted her chin to meet her eyes. "I will always come for you, but when you meet my brother, you should thank him." He shook his head. "It might have taken me a lot longer to find you if it hadn't been for him."

"Did I hear you mention me?" Cassidy turned to see a man who resembled Jordan in the doorway. He was clean shaven, wore glasses, and was dressed in a suit – about the polar opposite of Jordan – but the two shared the same strong jaw line.

"Of course he would hear that," Jordan muttered

under his breath as he pushed himself up from the bed. "Cassidy, this is my brother Graham. Graham, this is Cassidy."

Graham's eyebrow rose as he stepped forward and extended a hand. "The firefighter, right?"

But Cassidy had no intention of simply shaking his hand. She threw her arms around the man who froze in shock. "Thank you."

"Uh, you're welcome?" Graham said. "Wow, maybe you should get injured more often if it'll mean beautiful women throw themselves at me."

"Not on your life," Jordan said as he grabbed his wallet off the nearby table before returning to stand beside Cassidy.

Cassidy turned her face up to Jordan's, a teasing glint sparkling in her eyes. "So, I've met your brother. Are you hiding any other family members from me?"

Jordan raised an eyebrow at her as he put his arm around her and pulled her to his chest. "To be fair, I've been a little busy saving children and rescuing you from a stalker to ramble on about my family, but I'll be happy to tell you whatever you want to know."

Cassidy didn't think she had ever heard sweeter words. She wrapped her arm around his waist and smiled up at him. "I want to know everything."

THE EPILOGUE

"*A* few months ago, our father left us this building in his will, and I thought Graham was crazy to want to fix it up." The crowd cheered and clapped as Jordan tossed his brother a teasing grin. "But after taking some time off to heal and having to spend a lot of that time with my brother, I think he might have been right after all." Another cheer erupted and Jordan scanned the crowd. Many were firefighters who worked with Cassidy, some were paramedics or hospital staff, and the rest were cops.

Al caught his eye and nodded at him as she clapped. He'd been worried when he'd started seeing Cassidy, but Al had made it a point to let him know she was happy for him. For them. Perhaps she'd also realized dating a partner was not a good idea, or maybe she'd seen how perfect he and Cassidy were together. Regardless, he was thankful. He didn't want to lose Al as his partner

Jordan grinned as he returned her nod and wrapped his arm around Cassidy. He had never wanted this restaurant or the responsibility that went with it, but after spending the last few weeks fixing it up with Cassidy and Graham, it felt more like a second home than a responsibility.

And maybe that's why his father had kept it. Maybe he had seen how Graham and Jordan had drifted apart and how this project might bring them back together. It certainly would explain the posters in the walls. Perhaps, in a lucid moment, his father had walled up the posters knowing he would sell them and drink the money away if he didn't. Maybe his father hadn't even known about the posters in the walls. Jordan still didn't know how his father had acquired this building, but he supposed that part might just have to remain a mystery. For now. And he was okay with that.

"Thanks, big brother," Graham said taking over the announcing duty. "Ladies and gentlemen, Fire Dreams is officially open for business."

Fire Dreams. It might be an odd name for a restaurant, but it fit Jordan and Graham. So much of their dreams growing up had gone up in smoke, but fire held a cleansing power, and somehow this place also felt like a new beginning.

"You okay?" Cassidy asked as she laid a hand on his chest.

"Yeah, I was just thinking how I never saw myself here. Owning a restaurant, surrounded by firefighters, and in love with the prettiest one of them all."

Cassidy threw back her head and laughed. "Well, that's not hard considering the rest of them are men."

"That is a true statement, but I still think you're the prettiest one in here." He turned her to face him and let his hands slide down to her waist. "In fact, we might have to whip out one of those hoses because I feel the heat blaze every time I'm around you."

She rolled her eyes and batted his chest. "That might be the corniest line I've ever heard."

"But you still like me," he said as he lowered his face to hers and touched her lips.

"Yeah, I still like you," she breathed as his lips moved to her neck, "but I'm definitely going to have to work on your moves."

He pulled back and feigned a hurt expression. "There is nothing wrong with my moves. In fact, I almost forgot something." He stepped over to the bar and grabbed the rectangular box he had placed there earlier. "I got something for you."

"What? It's your opening night. I should have gotten something for you."

"Yeah, you should have, but you didn't. Maybe I need to work on your moves," he teased with a smile. "Open it." He placed the box in her hands and watched as she unwrapped the paper. He hoped she would like it. Most people might think it was just a trinket, but he suspected it would hold some significance for her.

She pulled off the top of the box and gasped. "Jordan, how did you? Where did you?" Her words trailed off as she pulled out the small license plate he'd had custom made for her. In the middle was her name and across the bottom was a row of flames.

"One of the guys who did the interior design has a custom trinket shop. I thought it was time you actually had something with your name on it."

Her eyes glistened as she met his gaze. "This is....thank you."

"See? I have good moves," he said pulling her close again.

"Yes, Officer Graves, it appears you do." She lifted her head and he wasted no time in claiming her lips once again.

"Help! Is there a doctor in here?"

Jordan pulled back and turned to see who needed assistance. A man stood in the doorway, a frantic look on his face.

"There was an accident. A woman's been injured, but the guy who hit her took off. She looks bad though. Are any of you doctors?"

"I am." Brody Cavanaugh fought his way through the crowd followed by two or three other people Jordan recognized from the hospital.

"We better go too," Jordan said grabbing the license plate and stashing it behind the bar once more before hurrying outside with Cassidy and the rest of the crowd.

The sun had set, but the streetlights illuminated the area and down the street they could see the car – a red sports car – folded in an accordion shape.

"Get the Jaws of Life," Bubba ordered as he sprinted towards the car. Around him, firemen spread out. Some ran toward the truck that was parked on the curb and others followed Bubba including Cassidy.

Jordan looked around for the man who had entered the bar. He stood a few feet away wringing his hands together. "You." Jordan hurried over to the man. "I'm Detective Graves. Did you see the accident happen?"

"It happened so fast. I heard the crash and then it sounded like he gunned it. Why would he gun it if he knew he'd hurt someone?" The man was rambling, clearly in shock.

"Can you tell me what the vehicle looked like that hit her?"

The man turned to face Jordan and for a moment his eyes were clear. "It was a truck. A black Ford truck."

Want to know who was in the accident and who was the driver of the truck? Find out the rest of the story in the riveting second book of the Men of Fire Beach series, Lost Dreams and New Beginnings coming soon.

THE END

IT'S NOT QUITE THE END!

Thank you so much for reading *Fire Games*. This book was originally planned to be the third full length book in the Blushing Brides series, but as it lent itself more to suspense, I decided to make it a spin off series. As you can see, there is more planned for The Men of Fire Beach and I hope you'll take that journey with me.

I hope you enjoyed the story as I really enjoyed writing it. If you did, would you do me a favor? If you did, please leave a review. It really helps. It doesn't have to be long - just a few words to help other readers know what they're getting.

I'd love to hear from you, not only about this story, but about the characters or stories you'd like read in the future. I'm always looking for new ideas and if I use one of your characters or stories, I'll send you a free ebook and paperback of the book with a special dedication. Write to me at loranahoopes@gmail.com. And if you'd like to see what's coming next, be sure to stop by authorloranahoopes.com

I also have a weekly newsletter that contains many wonderful things like pictures of my adorable children, chances to win awesome prizes, new releases and sales I might be holding, great books from other authors, and anything else that strikes my fancy and that I think you would enjoy. I'll even send you the first chapter of my newest (maybe not even released yet) book if you'd like to sign up.

Even better, I solemnly swear to only send out one newsletter a week (usually on Tuesday unless life gets in the way which with three kids it usually does). I will not spam you, sell your email address to solicitors or anyone else, or any of those other terrible things.

God Bless,
  Lorana

NOT READY TO SAY GOODBYE YET?

CASSIDY AND JORDAN will appear in the future novels, but the next book is going to focus on a doctor. I bet you can't guess who?

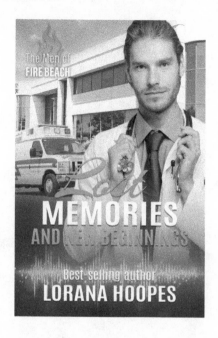

Lost Memories and New Beginnings

He's a doctor who's still grieving...

She's a patient with no memory...

Will they find love with each other or will her past keep them apart? ....

LOST MEMORIES PREVIEW

"Help! Is there a doctor in here?"

Dr. Brody Cavanaugh looked up from his sparkling water to the doorway to see what the commotion was. A man stood in the doorway, a frantic look on his face.

"There was an accident. A woman's been injured, but the guy who hit her took off. She looks bad though. Are any of you doctors?"

"I am." Brody caught fellow doctor Caleb Pearson's attention and pushed back from the table. His drink could wait. He and Pearson fought their way through the crowd and spilled out onto the street with the rest of the crowd following behind them.

The sun had set, but the streetlights illuminated the

area and down the street he could see the car – a red sports car – folded in an accordion shape.

"Get the Jaws of Life," one of the firemen ordered as he sprinted towards the car. Around Brody, firemen spread out. Some ran toward the truck that was parked on the curb and others the large fireman toward the car including Cassidy.

Brody approached the car and stood to the side watching as two large firemen worked the jaws of life to cut away the driver's door. The groaning sound of the metal snapping not only overpowered the roaring of the hydraulic tool but reminded him of nails on chalkboards, and he resisted the urge to place his hands on his ears. The red sports car was twisted in such an awkward shape that he feared the driver had been crushed in the crash.

Ivy Hopkins appeared beside him, her eyes wide and fixed to the scene. "Do you think she'll make it?" Her slender fingers pulled on the ends of her blonde hair.

"I don't know, but we'll do everything we can."

"Her legs are pinned under the dashboard," one of the men called out as the deafening sound of the hydraulic ceased momentarily. The sudden stillness was jarring. "We need the ram."

Two other firemen hurried forward with a different tool and after a moment, the hydraulic sound filled the night again.

"Okay, we've got her free."

That was his cue. The firemen stepped aside as he and Ivy stepped up to the car. Brody tried not to focus on the metallic scent of blood in the air or the mangled mess that was the woman's legs as he surveyed the scene closer.

Ivy checked for a pulse and then strapped on a neck collar. "She's breathing, but her vitals are weak." She unfastened the seat belt and moved it away from the woman. Then she switched places with him allowing him to snake his arms under the woman's arms and pull.

The woman's face and hair were coated in blood, and Brody thought some of the cuts on her face might need stitches, but that was not his immediate concern. No, his immediate concern was her legs. Particularly her right foot. It had been mangled badly in the crash and he just hoped that it had not been crushed. Crush injuries generally resulted in amputations, and though he knew they weren't the end of the world, he didn't like performing them if he didn't have to and especially not on someone so young.

"Whoa, I'm going to call ahead and tell them what's coming," Caleb said as he caught a glimpse of the woman.

Brody nodded as he and Ivy placed the woman on the gurney and loaded her up in the ambulance. They sat in the back with her as Rick, the other EMT, and Caleb climbed in the cab. Ivy set up an IV as Brody monitored the vitals and took a closer look at her feet.

"Is she going to lose them?" Ivy asked.

"I don't know, but they don't look good."

PRE-ORDER LOST MEMORIES.... Today

A FREE STORY FOR YOU

Enjoyed this story? Not ready to quit reading yet? If you sign up for my newsletter, you will receive The Billionaire's Impromptu Bet right away as my thank you gift for choosing to hang out with me.

The Billionaire's Impromptu Bet

A SWAT officer. A bored billionaire heiress. A bet that could change everything....

Read on for a taste of The Billionaire's Impromptu Bet....

THE BILLIONAIRE'S IMPROMPTU BET PREVIEW

*B*rie Carter fell back spread eagle on her queen-sized canopy bed sending her blonde hair fanning out behind her. With a large sigh, she uttered, "I'm bored."

"How can you be bored? You have like millions of dollars." Her friend, Ariel, plopped down in a seated position on the bed beside her and flicked her raven hair off her shoulder. "You want to go shopping? I hear Tiffany's is having a special right now."

Brie rolled her eyes. Shopping? Where was the excitement in that? With her three platinum cards, she could go shopping whenever she wanted. "No, I'm bored with shopping too. I have everything. I want to do something exciting. Something we don't normally do."

Brie enjoyed being rich. She loved the unlimited

credit cards at her disposal, the constant apparel of new clothes, and of course the penthouse apartment her father paid for, but lately, she longed for something more fulfilling.

Ariel's hazel eyes widened. "I know. There's a new bar down on Franklin Street. Why don't we go play a little game?"

Brie sat up, intrigued at the secrecy and the twinkle in Ariel's eyes. "What kind of game?"

"A betting game. You let me pick out any man in the place. Then you try to get him to propose to you."

Brie wrinkled her nose. "But I don't want to get married." She loved her freedom and didn't want to share her penthouse with anyone, especially some man.

"You don't marry him, silly. You just get him to propose."

Brie bit her lip as she thought. It had been awhile since her last relationship and having a man dote on her for a month might be interesting, but…. "I don't know. It doesn't seem very nice."

"How about I sweeten the pot? If you win, I'll set you up on a date with my brother."

Brie cocked her head. Was she serious? The only thing Brie couldn't seem to buy in the world was the affection of Ariel's very handsome, very wealthy, brother. He was a movie star, just the kind of person Brie could consider marrying in the future. She'd had a crush on him as long as she and Ariel had been friends, but he'd always seen her as just that, his little sister's friend. "I thought you didn't want me dating your brother."

"I don't." Ariel shrugged. "But he's between girlfriends right now, and I know you've wanted it for ages. If you win this bet, I'll set you up. I can't guarantee any more than one date though. The rest will be up to you."

Brie wasn't worried about that. Charm she possessed in abundance. She simply needed some alone time with him, and she was certain she'd be able to convince him they were meant to be together. "All right. You've got a deal."

Ariel smiled. "Perfect. Let's get you changed then and see who the lucky man will be.

A tiny tug pulled on Brie's heart that this still wasn't right, but she dismissed it. This was simply a means to an end, and he'd never have to know.

JESSE CALHOUN RELAXED as the rhythmic thudding of the speed bag reached his ears. Though he loved his job, it was stressful being the SWAT sniper. He hated having to take human lives and today had been especially rough. The team had been called out to a drug bust, and Jesse was forced to return fire at three hostiles. He didn't care that they fired at his team and himself first. Taking a life was always hard, and every one of them haunted his dreams.

"You gonna bust that one too?" His co-worker Brendan appeared by his side. Brendan was the opposite of Jesse in nearly every way. Where Jesse's hair was a dark copper, Brendan's was nearly black. Jesse sported paler skin and a dusting of freckles across his nose, but Brendan's skin was naturally dark and freckle free.

Jesse flashed a crooked grin, but kept his eyes on the small, swinging black bag. The speed bag was his way to release, but a few times he had started hitting while still too keyed up and he had ruptured the bag. Okay, five times, but who was counting really? Besides, it was a better way to calm his nerves than other things he could choose. Drinking, fights, gambling, women.

"Nah, I think this one will last a little longer." His shoulders began to burn, and he gave the bag another few punches for good measure before dropping his arms and letting it swing to a stop. "See? It lives to be hit at least another day." Every once in a while, Jesse missed training the way he used to. Before he joined the force, he had been an amateur boxer, on his way to being a pro, but a shoulder injury had delayed his training and forced him to consider something else. It had eventually healed, but by then he had lost his edge.

"Hey, why don't you come drink with us?" Brendan

clapped a hand on Jesse's shoulder as they headed into the locker room.

"You know I don't drink." Jesse often felt like the outsider of the team. While half of the six-man team was married, the other half found solace in empty bottles and meaningless relationships. Jesse understood that - their job was such that they never knew if they would come home night after night - but he still couldn't partake.

Brendan opened his locker and pulled out a clean shirt. He peeled off his current one and added deodorant before tugging on the new one. "You don't have to drink. Look, I won't drink either. Just come and hang out with us. You have no one waiting for you at home."

That wasn't entirely true. Jesse had Bugsy, his Boston Terrier, but he understood Brendan's point. Most days, Jesse went home, fed Bugsy, made dinner, and fell asleep watching TV on the couch. It wasn't much of a life. "All right, I'll go, but I'm not drinking."

Brendan's lips pulled back to reveal his perfectly white teeth. He bragged about them, but Jesse knew they were veneers. "That's the spirit. Hurry up and change. We don't want to leave the rest of the team waiting."

"Is everyone coming?" Jesse pulled out his shower necessities. Brendan might feel comfortable going out with just a new application of deodorant, but Jesse needed to wash more than just dirt and sweat off. He needed to wash the sound of the bullets and the sight of lifeless bodies from his mind.

"Yeah, Pat's wife is pregnant again and demanding some crazy food concoctions. Pat agreed to pick them up if she let him have an hour. Cam and Jared's wives are having a girls' night, so the whole gang can be together. It will be nice to hang out when we aren't worried about being shot at."

"Fine. Give me ten minutes. Unlike you, I like to clean up before I go out."

Brendan smirked. "I've never had any complaints. Besides, do you know how long it takes me to get my hair like this?"

Jesse shook his head as he walked into the shower, but he knew it was true. Brendan had rugged good looks and muscles to match. He rarely had a hard time finding a woman. Jesse on the other hand hadn't dated anyone in the last few months. It wasn't that he hadn't been looking, but he was quieter than his teammates. And he wasn't looking for right now. He was looking for forever. He just hadn't found it yet.

Click here to continue reading The Billionaire's Impromptu Bet.

THE STORY DOESN'T END!

You've met a few people and fallen in love....

I bet you're wondering how you can meet everyone else.

Star Lake Series:

When Love Returns: The first in the Star Lake series. Presley Hays and Brandon Scott were best friends in High School until Morgan entered their town and stole Brandon's heart. Devastated, Presley takes a scholarship to Le Cordon Bleu, but five years later, she is back in Star Lake after a tough breakup. Brandon thought he'd never return to Star Lake after Morgan left him and his daughter Joy, but when his father needs help, he returns home and finds more than he bargained for. Can Presley and Brandon forget past hurts or will their stubborn natures keep them apart forever?

Once Upon a Star: The second book in the Star Lake series. Audrey left Star Lake to pursue acting, but after an unplanned pregnancy her jobs and her money dwindled, leaving her no option except to return home and start over. Blake was the quintessential nerd in high school and was never able to tell Audrey how he felt. Now that he's gained confidence and some muscle, will he finally be able to reveal his feelings? Once Upon a Star will take you back to Christmas in Star Lake. Revisit your favorite characters and meet a few ones in this sweet Christmas read.

Love Conquers All: Lanie Perkins Hall never imagined being divorced at thirty. Nor did she imagine falling for an old friend, but when she runs into Azarius Jacobson, she can't deny the attraction. As they begin to spend more time together, Lanie struggles with the fact Azarius keeps his past a secret. What is he hiding? And will she ever be able to get him to open up? Azarius Jacobson has loved Lanie Perkins Hall from the moment he saw her, but issues from his past have left him guarded. Now that he has another chance with her, will he find the courage to share his life with her? Or will his emotional walls create a barrier that will leave him alone once more? Find out in this heartfelt, emotional third book (stand alone) in the Star Lake series.

The Heartbeats Series:

Where It All Began: Sandra Baker thought her life was on the right track until she ended up pregnant. Her boyfriend, not wanting the baby, pushes her to have an abortion. After the procedure, Sandra's life falls apart, and she turns to alcohol. Her relationship ends, and she struggles to find meaning in her life. When she meets Henry Dobbs, a strong Christian man, she begins to wonder if God would accept her. Will she tell Henry her darkest secret? And will she ever be able to forgive herself and find healing? Find out in this emotional love story.

The Power of Prayer: Callie Green thought she had her whole life planned out until her fiance left her at the altar. When her carefully laid plans crumble, she begins to make mistakes at work and engage in uncharacteristic activities. After a mistake nearly costs her her job, she cashes in her honeymoon tickets for some time away. There she meets JD, a charming Christian man who, even though she is not a believer, captures her interest. Before their relationship can deepen, Callie's ex-fiance shows back up in her life and she is forced to choose between Daniel and JD. Who will she choose and how will her choice affect the rest of her life? Find out in this touching novel.

When Hearts Collide: Amanda Adams has always been a Christian, but she's a novice at relationships. When she meets Caleb, her emotions get the best of her and she ignores the sign that something is amiss. Will she find out before it's too late? Jared Masterson is still healing from his girlfriend's strange rejection and disappearance when he meets Amanda. She captivates his heart, but can he save her from making the biggest mistake of her life? A must read for mothers and daughters. Though part of the series and the first of the college spin off series, it is a stand alone book and can be read separately.

A Past Forgiven: Jess Peterson has lived a life of abuse and lost her self worth, but when she is paired with a Christian roommate, she begins to wonder if there is a loving father looking down on her. Her decisions lead her one way, but when she ends up pregnant, she must make some major changes. Chad Michelson is healing from his own past and uses meaningless relationships to hide his pain, but when Jess becomes pregnant, he begins to wonder about the meaning of life. Can he step up and be there for Jess and the baby?

Sweet Billionaires Series:

The Billionaire's Secret: Maxwell Banks was the ultimate player until he found himself caring for a daughter he didn't know he had. Can he change to become the role model she needs? Alyssa Miller hasn't had the best luck with past relationships, so why is she falling for the one man who is sure to break her heart?

Though nearly complete opposites, feelings develop, but can Max really change his philandering ways? Or will one mistake seal his fate forever?

A Brush with a Billionaire: Brent just wanted to finish his novel in peace, but when his car breaks down in Sweet Grove, he is forced to deal with a female mechanic and try to get along. Sam thought she had given up on city boys, but when Brent shows up in her shop, she finds herself fighting attraction. Will their stubborn natures keep them apart or can a small town festival bring them together?

The Billionaire's Christmas Miracle: Drew Devonshire is captivated by the woman he meets at a masquerade ball, but who is she? Gwen Rodgers is a teacher, but when she pretends to be her friend and meets Drew at a masquerade ball, her world gets thrown upside down.

The Billionaire's Cowboy Groom: Carrie Bliss finally found the man she wants to marry but there's just one little problem. She's technically still married. Cal Roper hasn't seen her in years but his heart still belongs to his wife. When she returns to town requesting a divorce, can he convince her they belong together?

The Cowboy Billionaire: Coming Soon!

The Lawkeeper Series:
Lawfully Matched: Kate Whidby doesn't want to

impose on her newly married brother after their parents die, so she accepts a mail order bride offer in the paper. Little does she know the man she intends to marry has a dark past, sending her fleeing into a neighboring town and into Jesse Jenning's life. Jesse never wanted to be in law enforcement, but after a band of robbers kills his fiancee, he dons the badge and swears revenge. Will he find his fiancee's killer? And when Kate flies into his life, will he be able to put his painful past behind him in order to love again?

Lawfully Justified: William Cook turns to bounty hunting after losing his wife. When he suffers a life-threatening injury, he is forced to stay in town with an intriguing woman. Emma Stewart has moved back in with her widowed father, the town doctor, but she still longs for a family of her own, so no one is more surprised than she is when she starts to develop feeling for the bounty hunter, who hides his heart of gold behind a rugged exterior. Can Emma offer William a reason to stay? Can William find a way to heal from his broken past to start a future with Emma? Or will a haunting secret take away all the possibilities of this budding romance?

The Scarlet Wedding: William and Emma are planning their wedding, but an outbreak and a return from his past force them to change their plans. Is a happily ever after still in their future?

Lawfully Redeemed: Dani Higgins is a K9 cop looking to make a name for herself, but she finds herself at the mercy of a stranger after an accident. Calvin Phillips just wanted to help his brother, but somehow he ended up in the middle of a police investigation and caring for the woman trying to bring his brother in.

The Still Small Voice Series:

The Still Small Voice: Jordan Wright was searching for something after she gave her son up for adoption. What she found was God, and she began receiving visions. But can she trust Him when he asks her to do something big? Kat Jameson had long been a lukewarm Christian, but when her friend dies and she begins seeing lights, she thinks she is going crazy. Then she meets someone with a message for her. Will she be able to give up control and do what is asked of her?

A Spark in the Darkness coming soon!

Blushing Brides Series:

The Cowboy's Reality Bride: Tyler Hall just wanted to find love, but the women he dated wanted more than his small-town life provided. He gets more than he bargained for when he ends up on a reality dating show and falls for a woman who is not a contestant. Laney Swann has been running from her past for years, but it takes meeting a man on a reality dating show to make her see there's no need to run.

The Reality Bride's Baby: Laney wants nothing more than a baby, but when she starts feeling dizzy is it pregnancy or something more serious?

The Producer's Unlikely Bride: Justin Miller had given up on love, but when his image needs help, he finds himself needing the aid of a stranger who just happens to be a romance writer. Ava McDermott is waiting for the perfect love, but after agreeing to a fake relationship with Justin, she finds herself falling for real.

Ava's Blessing in Disguise: Five years after marriage, Ava faces a mysterious illness that threatens to ruin her career. Will she find out what it is?

The Soldier's Steadfast Bride: coming soon

The Men of Fire Beach

Fire Games: Cassidy returns home from Who Wants to Marry a Cowboy to find obsessive letters from a fan. The cop assigned to help her wants to get back to his case, but what she sees at a fire may just be the key he's looking for.

Lost Memories and New Beginnings: coming soon

Stand Alones:

Love Renewed: This books is part of the multi

author second chance series. When fate reunites high school sweethearts separated by life's choices, can they find a second chance at love at a snowy lodge amid a little mystery?

Her children's early reader chapter book series:
    The Wishing Stone #1: Dangerous Dinosaur
    The Wishing Stone #2: Dragon Dilemma
    The Wishing Stone #3: Mesmerizing Mermaids
    The Wishing Stone #4: Pyramid Puzzle
    The Wishing Stone Inspirations 1: Mary's Miracle
    To see a list of all her books

authorloranahoopes.com
loranahoopes@gmail.com

DISCUSSION QUESTIONS

1. What was your favorite scene in the book? What made it your favorite?

2. Did you have a favorite line in the book? What do you think made it so memorable?

3. Who was your favorite character in the book and why?

4. When did you know who the stalker was?

5. What do you think would be the hardest part about being on a reality dating show?

6. What did you learn about God from reading this book?

7. How can you use that knowledge in your life from now on?

8. What can you take away from Cassidy's and Jordan's relationship?

9. What do you think would make the story even better?

ABOUT THE AUTHOR

Lorana Hoopes is an inspirational author originally from Texas but now living in the PNW with her husband and three children. When not writing, she can be seen kickboxing at the gym, singing, or acting on stage. One day, she hopes to retire from teaching and write full time.